準備多益口説測驗，一石二鳥

　　從前，面對紙上的英語檢定考試，同學只要勤寫測驗題庫，就能拿到不錯的分數。但是現在，為了更精確地測出考生的英文能力，英語檢定考試加考口說與寫作，已是必然的趨勢。

　　全世界，超過 8000 家企業、學校及政府採用的「多益測驗」，於 2008 年推出新制「多益」。其中最令考生恐慌的一項變革，就是要加考「口說」。有鑑於此，「學習出版公司」針對「多益口說測驗」做了徹底的研究，出版「**多益口説測驗**」一書，相信對考生會有很大的幫助。

　　本書共有八回，每一回都是一個完整的測驗，題型與「多益口說測驗」完全相同，考生可以多加練習，考試時必能有高水準的表現。題目後面的「答題範例」，完全以「**一口氣英語**」的方式，**三句一組，九句一段，容易背，不容易忘記。**

　　全世界的人，學英語最大的困難，就是學了不會說。同學不妨把口說考試當作是一個助力，激勵你學好英語會話。我們不只要背答題範例，還要背到變成直覺，只要把九句背至五秒鐘內，就終生不會忘記。準備了「多益口說測驗」，實際上也學會了說英語會話，一石二鳥。

　　本書另附 MP3，每回測驗有兩個音軌。第一個音軌是完全仿照考試情況，播放試題並留時間給同學作答，同學可以以此做模擬練習。第二個音軌是答題範例，由專業的美籍播音員錄製，同學跟著唸，模仿他們的語調，說起英文來就會像道地的美國人。

　　本書在編審及校對的每一階段，均力求完善，但仍恐有疏漏之處，誠盼各界先進不吝指正。

劉　毅

「TOEIC 口說測驗」簡介

1. 什麼是「TOEIC 口說測驗」?

「TOEIC 測驗」是 ETS（美國教育測驗服務社）策劃的測驗之一。目的在評量個人在職場及日常生活中，使用英文做溝通的能力。

而「TOEIC 口說測驗」是 ETS 新推出的測驗。以往，傳統的「TOEIC 測驗」只考聽力和閱讀，但隨著全球化和網路化的時代來臨，進行商務活動時，舉凡寫電子郵件、做視訊會議、洽談公事等等，使用英語口說及寫作的機會，愈來愈頻繁。為因應這樣的趨勢，ETS 新增了「TOEIC 口說與寫作測驗」，俾使「TOEIC 測驗」，能更為有效地評量出考生聽、說、讀、寫四方面的英語能力。

2. TOEIC 口說測驗題型說明

題號	內　　　容	說　　　明	準備時間	作答時間
1-2	Read a text aloud 朗讀一段文章	朗讀一段英文短文	45 秒	45 秒
3	Describe a picture 描述圖片	描述螢幕上的照片內容	30 秒	45 秒
4-6	Respond to questions 回答問題	依據題目設定的情境，回答與日常生活有關的問題	無	15 秒 / 30 秒
7-9	Respond to questions using information provided 依據題目資料應答	依據題目設定的情境與提供的資料回答問題	無	15 秒 / 30 秒
10	Propose a solution 提出解決方案	依據題目設定的情境，針對問題點提出對策	30 秒	60 秒
11	Express an opinion 陳述意見	針對指定的議題陳述意見並提出理由	15 秒	60 秒

3. TOEIC 口說測驗評分標準

前四個題型（Questions 1-9）採 0～3 分的評分級距，後兩個題型（Questions 10-11）採 0～5 分的評分級距。之後再透過統計程序，將各大題的得分換算爲 0～200 分。這 0～200 分又對應到八個能力等級，其對應關係如下：

分　　數	等　　級	分　　數	等　　級
190-200	8	80-100	4
160-180	7	60-70	3
130-150	6	40-50	2
110-120	5	0-30	1

4. TOEIC 口說測驗的施測方式爲何？

TOEIC 口說爲網路型態的測驗（Internet-based test），試題會經由網路傳到考生的電腦上。每位考生皆有一副耳機，上面連著一個麥克風。考試時，題目會出現在電腦上，耳機中也會播放作答指導或題目。考生作答的內容將以數位方式錄音，而後傳送到 ETS 的線上評分網路系統，由評分人員進行評分。

TOEIC 口說測驗與寫作測驗是一起考的。兩項測驗的報名及施測程序，都是一起進行。考完口說測驗後，沒有休息時間，緊接著就進行寫作測驗，全程歷時約 1.5 小時。

※ 報名請洽：

ETS 台灣區代表　忠欣股份有限公司

（106）台北市復興南路二段 45 號 2 樓

（106）台北郵政 26-585 號信箱

TEL: (02) 2701-7333　FAX: (02) 2755-2822

Website: www.toeic.com.tw

E-mail: service@toeic.com.tw

TOEIC Speaking Test ①

Question 1: Read a Text Aloud

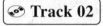 **Track 02**

Directions: In this part of the test, you will read aloud the text on the screen. You will have 45 seconds to prepare. Then you will have 45 seconds to read the text aloud.

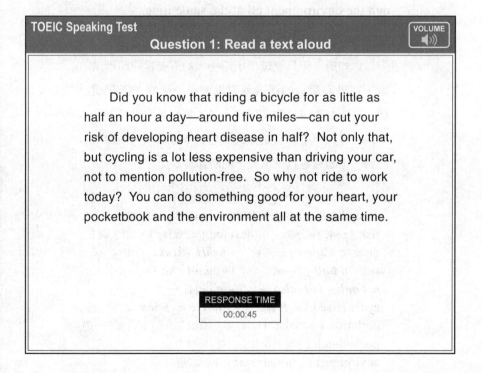

TOEIC Speaking Test

Question 1: Read a text aloud

VOLUME

Did you know that riding a bicycle for as little as half an hour a day—around five miles—can cut your risk of developing heart disease in half? Not only that, but cycling is a lot less expensive than driving your car, not to mention pollution-free. So why not ride to work today? You can do something good for your heart, your pocketbook and the environment all at the same time.

RESPONSE TIME
00:00:45

題目解說 (⊘ **Track 03**)

Did you know that riding a bicycle for as little as half an hour a day—around five miles—can cut your risk of developing heart disease in half? Not only that, but cycling is a lot less expensive than driving your car, not to mention pollution-free. So why not ride to work today? You can do something good for your heart, your pocketbook and the environment all at the same time.

你知道一天只要騎半小時—大約五英里—的腳踏車，罹患心臟病的風險就可以減少一半嗎？不只這樣，騎腳踏車還比開車便宜多了，更別說它零污染。所以，今天何不騎腳踏車去上班呢？這樣做，對你的心臟、你的錢包以及環境，同時都有好處。

** ————————————————————

around〔ə'raʊnd〕adv. 大約　　　cut〔kʌt〕v. 減少

risk〔rɪsk〕n. 風險　　　develop〔dɪ'vɛləp〕v. 患（病）

disease〔dɪ'ziz〕n. 疾病　　　*heart disease* 心臟病

cut…in half 把…減少一半（= *cut…by half*）

not only…but (also)~ 不僅…，而且~

cycle〔'saɪkḷ〕v. 騎腳踏車　　　***not to mention*** 更不用說

pollution〔pə'luʃən〕n. 污染　　free〔fri〕adj. 沒有…的

pocketbook〔'pɑkɪt,bʊk〕n. 錢包

environment〔ɪn'vaɪrənmənt〕n. 環境

at the same time 同時

Question 2: Read a Text Aloud

 **Track 02**

Directions: In this part of the test, you will read aloud the text on the screen. You will have 45 seconds to prepare. Then you will have 45 seconds to read the text aloud.

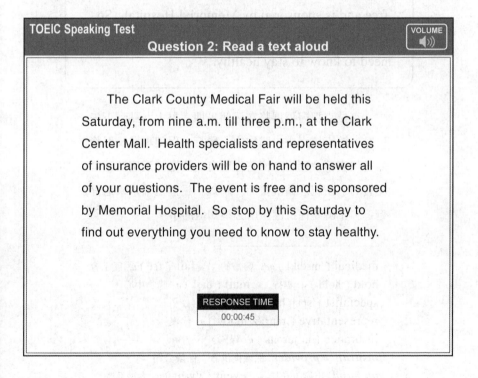

TOEIC Speaking Test

VOLUME

Question 2: Read a text aloud

The Clark County Medical Fair will be held this Saturday, from nine a.m. till three p.m., at the Clark Center Mall. Health specialists and representatives of insurance providers will be on hand to answer all of your questions. The event is free and is sponsored by Memorial Hospital. So stop by this Saturday to find out everything you need to know to stay healthy.

RESPONSE TIME
00:00:45

題目解說 (☉ **Track 03**)

> The Clark County Medical Fair will be held this Saturday, from nine a.m. till three p.m., at the Clark Center Mall. Health specialists and representatives of insurance providers will be on hand to answer all of your questions. The event is free and is sponsored by Memorial Hospital. So stop by this Saturday to find out everything you need to know to stay healthy.

克拉克郡醫療展將在這個星期六早上九點到下午三點，於克拉克中央購物中心舉行。保健專家及保險公司代表都會到場，回答你所有的問題。這個活動是免費的，由紀念醫院贊助。所以，這個禮拜六來這裡逛逛，了解要保持健康所必須知道的事。

** ───────────────

medical〔'mɛdɪkḷ〕*adj.* 醫療的　　fair〔fɛr〕*n.* 展示會
hold〔hold〕*v.* 舉行　　mall〔mɔl〕*n.* 購物中心
specialist〔'spɛʃəlɪst〕*n.* 專家
representative〔ˌrɛprɪ'zɛntətɪv〕*n.* 代表
insurance〔ɪn'ʃurəns〕*n.* 保險
insurance provider 保險提供者；保險公司
on hand 出席；在場　　event〔ɪ'vɛnt〕*n.* 大型活動
free〔fri〕*adj.* 免費的　　sponsor〔'spɑnsə〕*v.* 贊助
memorial〔mə'morɪəl〕*adj.* 紀念的　　***stop by*** 順道拜訪
find out 發現；查明　　stay〔ste〕*v.* 保持

Question 3: Describe a Picture

Track 02

Directions: In this part of the test, you will describe the picture on your screen in as much detail as you can. You will have 30 seconds to prepare your response. Then you will have 45 seconds to speak about the picture.

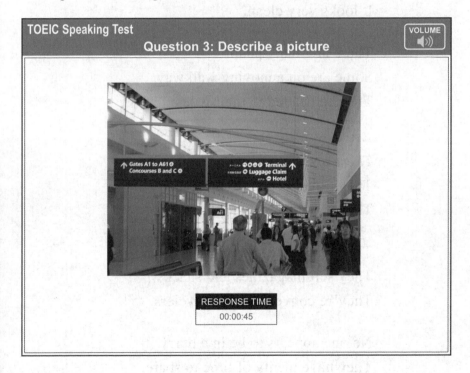

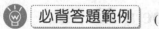 必背答題範例 (☛ **Track 03**)

This is an airport.
It's a picture of a terminal.
It looks like a large one.

It's a long narrow hall.
It's brightly lit.
It looks very clean.

There are many people.
Some are on a moving walkway.
They're headed to their gates.

There are many signs.
They direct people to the gates.
They show the way to the hotel.

There are some shops, too.
They sell magazines and snacks.
They're convenient for travelers.

No one appears to be in a hurry.
They have plenty of time to spare.
They're relaxed and happy.

中文翻譯

> **這是機場。**
> 這是航空站的照片。
> 看起來是座很大的航空站。
>
> 這是條長而狹窄的走廊。
> 光線很充足。
> 看起來非常乾淨。
>
> 有很多人。
> 有些在電動走道上。
> 他們正前往他們的登機門。
>
> **有很多標誌。**
> 它們引導人們前往登機門。
> 它們指出前往旅館的方向。
>
> 還有一些商店。
> 它們販賣雜誌和點心。
> 它們對旅客來說很方便。
>
> 沒有人顯得匆忙。
> 他們有很多多餘的時間。
> 他們輕鬆而愉快。

**

terminal〔ˈtɜmənḷ〕*n.* 航空站	hall〔hɔl〕*n.* 走廊
brightly〔ˈbraɪtlɪ〕*adv.* 明亮地	light〔laɪt〕*v.* 照亮
moving〔ˈmuvɪŋ〕*adj.* 移動的	walkway〔ˈwɔkˏwe〕*n.* 走道
be headed to 朝⋯方向前進	gate〔get〕*n.* 登機門
sign〔saɪn〕*n.* 標誌；告示	direct〔dəˈrɛkt〕*v.* 指引
in a hurry 匆忙	**plenty of** 很多
to spare 多餘的	relaxed〔rɪˈlækst〕*adj.* 放鬆的

Questions 4-6: Respond to Questions

Track 02

Directions: In this part of the test, you will answer three questions. For each question, begin responding immediately after you hear a beep. No preparation time is provided. You will have 15 seconds to respond to Questions 4 and 5 and 30 seconds to respond to Question 6.

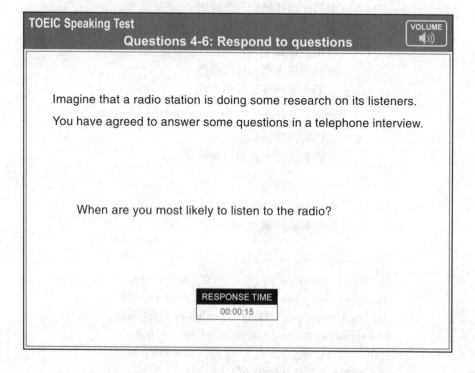

TOEIC Speaking Test
Questions 4-6: Respond to questions

VOLUME

Imagine that a radio station is doing some research on its listeners. You have agreed to answer some questions in a telephone interview.

When are you most likely to listen to the radio?

RESPONSE TIME
00:00:15

⇨ Question 5 is on the next page.

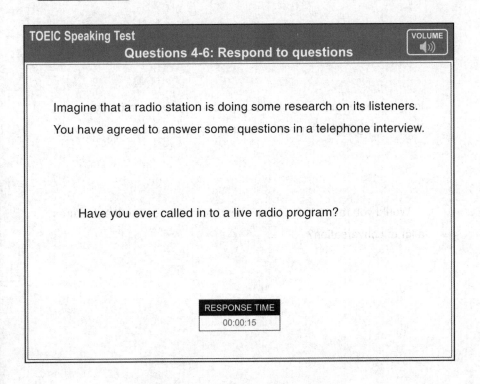

Track 02

TOEIC Speaking Test
Questions 4-6: Respond to questions

VOLUME

Imagine that a radio station is doing some research on its listeners.
You have agreed to answer some questions in a telephone interview.

Have you ever called in to a live radio program?

RESPONSE TIME
00:00:15

⇨ Question 6 is on the next page.

 Track 02

TOEIC Speaking Test
Questions 4-6: Respond to questions

VOLUME

Imagine that a radio station is doing some research on its listeners.
You have agreed to answer some questions in a telephone interview.

Would you rather listen to an all-music station or one that features
a lot of conversation?

RESPONSE TIME
00:00:30

必背答題範例 (Track 03)

Imagine that a radio station is doing some research on its listeners. You have agreed to answer some questions in a telephone interview.

想像一下，有家廣播電台正在對聽眾進行調查。你已同意於電話訪問中回答一些問題。

Q4: When are you most likely to listen to the radio?
你最有可能在何時聽廣播？

A4: I usually listen when I'm in the car.
我通常在車子裡聽廣播。
It makes traffic jams more fun.
這讓塞車時多了一點樂趣。
The DJs can also make me laugh.
DJ 也會令我發笑。

Q5: Have you ever called in to a live radio program?
你是否曾打電話到現場直播的廣播節目？

A5: Once I called to request a song. 我曾經打去點歌。
It was for my girlfriend's birthday.
那是為了我女朋友生日點的。
She was thrilled. 她很興奮。

** ──────────

imagine〔ɪˈmædʒɪn〕v. 想像　　*radio station* 廣播電台
research〔rɪsɝtʃ〕n. 調查　　interview〔ˈɪntɚ͵vju〕n. 訪問
a traffic jam 交通阻塞
DJ （電台的）音樂節目主持人（= *disk jockey*）
live〔laɪv〕adj. 現場的　　request〔rɪˈkwɛst〕v. 請求
request a song 點播歌曲　　thrilled〔θrɪld〕adj. 興奮的

Q6: Would you rather listen to an all-music station or one that features a lot of conversation?

你喜歡收聽只播音樂的電台，還是以講話爲主的電台？

A6: I turn on the radio mostly for the music.
I like pop and hip-hop the best.
I want to hear the latest tunes.

But I also like the DJs.
I like to hear their opinions.
I also like their funny jokes.

But I rarely listen to talk radio.
I just want to relax.
I don't want to listen to the news.

我打開收音機多半是爲了聽音樂。
我最喜歡流行音樂及嘻哈音樂。
我想要聽最新的歌曲。

但我也喜歡那些 DJ。
我喜歡聽他們的見解。
我也喜歡他們有趣的笑話。

不過我很少聽談話性節目。
我只想要放鬆。
我不想聽新聞。

**

rather〔'ræðɚ〕*adv.* 寧願　feature〔'fitʃɚ〕*v.* 以⋯爲特色
turn on 打開　mostly〔'mostlɪ〕*adv.* 多半
pop〔pɑp〕*n.* 流行音樂　hip-hop〔'hɪp'hɑp〕*n.* 嘻哈音樂
latest〔'letɪst〕*adj.* 最新的　tune〔tjun〕*n.* 曲調
opinion〔ə'pɪnjən〕*n.* 見解　funny〔'fʌnɪ〕*adj.* 好笑的
rarely〔'rɛrlɪ〕*adv.* 很少　***talk radio*** 談話性節目

Questions 7-9: Respond to Questions Using Information Provided

Track 02

TOEIC Speaking Test
Questions 7-9: Respond to questions using information provided

VOLUME

Directions: In this part of the test, you will answer three questions based on the information provided. You will have 30 seconds to read the information before the questions begin. For each question, begin responding immediately after you hear a beep. No additional preparation time is provided. You will have 15 seconds to respond to Questions 7 and 8 and 30 seconds to respond to Question 9.

Oak Park Community Board Meeting

When: 7 p.m., Wednesday, April 12

Where: Oak Park Community Center

Topic: Widening Oak Park Road

There are strong feelings both for and against the plan. Representatives of both sides will present their views. The discussion will be followed by a vote on whether or not the community should approve the plan.

➤ **County Commissioner Leslie Brown** is for the plan. She will speak about the number of new residents in the area and the increased traffic.

➤ **Bill Riley** is against the plan. He will present the concerns that residents have about the disruption to daily life and the impact on the environment.

➤ **David Park**, an engineer from the construction company, will give us information on how long the project will take to complete.

題目解說

【中文翻譯】

橡樹公園社區委員會會議

時間：四月十二日星期三，晚上七點
地點：橡樹公園社區中心
主題：拓寬橡樹公園路

對於這項計畫，有強烈贊成及反對的意見。雙方代表將會提出他們的看法。在討論過後，會投票表決社區是否應核准這項計畫。

➤ **郡政委員雷絲麗・布朗**贊成這項計畫。她將會談到這個地區新居民的人數，以及增加的交通量。

➤ **比爾・萊里**反對這項計畫。他將提出居民們對於日常生活受到干擾的憂慮，以及對環境的衝擊。

➤ **大衛・帕克**，建設公司的工程師，會告訴我們完成工程所需時間的資訊。

【背景敘述】

> Hi! This is Rose Wilson. I just moved to Oak Park and I'd like to get involved in the community. I heard that there's going to be a meeting next week, but I don't know the details. Can I ask you a few questions?

　　嗨！我是蘿絲·威爾森。我剛搬到橡樹公園，我想參與社區的事情。我聽說下週將會有一場會議，但我不清楚細節。我可以問你一些問題嗎？

**

oak〔ok〕*n.* 橡樹　　community〔kə'mjunətɪ〕*n.* 社區

board〔bord〕*n.* 委員會　　meeting〔'mitɪŋ〕*n.* 會議

widen〔'waɪdn̩〕*v.* 加寬　　feeling〔'filɪŋ〕*n.* 看法；感想

for〔fɔr〕*prep.* 贊成　　against〔ə'gɛnst〕*prep.* 反對

representative〔‚rɛprɪ'zɛntətɪv〕*n.* 代表

present〔prɪ'zɛnt〕*v.* 提出　　view〔vju〕*n.* 看法；觀點

be followed by 接著就是　　vote〔vot〕*n.* 投票

approve〔ə'pruv〕*v.* 批准　　***county commissioner*** 郡政委員

resident〔'rɛzədənt〕*n.* 居民　　traffic〔'træfɪk〕*n.* 交通量

concern〔kən'sɝn〕*n.* 擔憂；憂慮

disruption〔dɪs'rʌpʃən〕*n.* 中斷；混亂

impact〔'ɪmpækt〕*n.* 衝擊；影響　　engineer〔‚ɛndʒə'nɪr〕*n.* 工程師

construction〔kən'strʌkʃən〕*n.* 建設

information〔‚ɪnfɚ'meʃən〕*n.* 資訊

complete〔kəm'plit〕*v.* 完成　　move〔muv〕*v.* 搬家

get involved in 參與　　detail〔'ditel〕*n.* 細節

必背答題範例 (Track 03)

Q7: When is the meeting going to be held and
what time will it start?

請問會議將於何時舉行，幾點開始？

A7: It's on April twelfth.
That's next Wednesday.
It'll start at seven.

在四月十二日。

那是下個禮拜三。

將會在七點開始。

Q8: I heard there's going to be a vote. Do you
know what it's about?

我聽說將會有投票。請問你知道那和什麼有關嗎？

A8: There's a plan to widen Oak Park Road.
Some people think it's a good idea.
Others are against it.

有個拓寬橡樹公園路的計畫。

有些人認爲這是個好主意。

其他人反對。

** others〔ˈʌðəz〕*pron. pl.* 其他的人

Q9: Who is going to speak at the meeting?
誰會在會議中發言呢？

A9: Leslie Brown will speak.
She is a county commissioner.
She is for the plan.

Then Bill Riley will speak.
He's against the plan.
He's worried about the impact on the
environment.

Last will be David Park.
He's an engineer from the construction
company.
He'll tell us how long the project will take
to complete.

雷絲麗・布朗會發言。
她是郡政委員。
她支持這項計畫。

然後比爾・萊里會發言。
他反對這個計畫。
他擔心對環境的衝擊。

最後是大衛・帕克。
他是來自建設公司的工程師。
他會告訴我們這項計畫要花多久才能完成。

**

---

worried〔'wɜɪd〕*adj.* 擔心的

Question 10: Propose a Solution

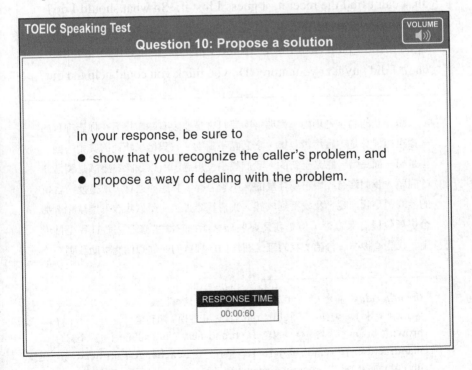

Track 02

Directions: In this part of the test, you will be presented with a problem and asked to propose a solution. You will have 30 seconds to prepare. Then you will have 60 seconds to speak. In your response, be sure to show that you recognize the problem, and propose a way of dealing with the problem.

TOEIC Speaking Test	VOLUME
Question 10: Propose a solution	

In your response, be sure to
- show that you recognize the caller's problem, and
- propose a way of dealing with the problem.

RESPONSE TIME
00:00:60

➡ Now listen to the voice message.

題目解說

【語音留言】

> Hi. My name is Marge Jefferson. I'm calling about something I bought in your store the other day. It's a toaster, and it's just not working right. It browns the bread on one side but not the other. It's brand-new. We've hardly used it, so I think the problem must be with the manufacturer. We didn't break it or anything. Anyway, I'd like to return it or exchange it for a new one. The problem is I, uh, I can't find the receipt. I guess I lost it. So what should I do? The toaster came with a guarantee, but I need the receipt to get it fixed. And I paid cash for it. Could I just exchange it for another one? I did buy it at your store. Do you think you could help me out?

嗨，我的名字是瑪姬・傑弗遜。我打來是要說有關前幾天在你店裡買的一樣東西。那是一台烤麵包機，它有點不對勁。它只烤了吐司的其中一面，但是另一面沒烤。它是全新的。我們幾乎沒用過，所以我認為應該是製造商的問題。我們沒有弄壞它或什麼的。不管怎樣，我想要退貨，或是換一台新的。問題是我，呃，我找不到收據。我猜我弄丟了。所以我該怎麼辦呢？那台烤麵包機有保證書，但是我需要收據才能把它拿去修理。而且我是付現金。我能直接換一台嗎？我的確是在你們店裡買的。你想你能幫助我嗎？

**

the other day 前幾天　　toaster (ˈtostɚ) *n.* 烤麵包機
work (wɝk) *v.* 運作　　right (raɪt) *adv.* 正確地；順利地
brown (braʊn) *v.* 將…烤成褐色　　brand-new (ˈbrændˈnju) *adj.* 全新的
manufacturer (ˌmænjəˈfæktʃərɚ) *n.* 製造商　　exchange (ɪksˈtʃendʒ) *v.* 更換
uh (ʌ) *interj.* 呃　　receipt (rɪˈsit) *n.* 收據　　*come with* 附有
guarantee (ˌgærənˈti) *n.* 保證書　　*help sb. out* 幫助某人

 必背答題範例 (Track 03)

I'm sure I can help you.
Don't worry.
I'll do whatever I can.

We'll take full responsibility.
Our products are high quality.
But occasionally there are problems.

If it's broken, you can return it.
No questions asked.
We'll replace it right away.

A receipt would make it easier.
It's an important document.
Next time, put it in a safe place.

I can't give you a cash refund.
For that you need a receipt.
But we'll make sure you're happy.

Just bring the toaster back to the store.
We'll take it back.
We'll give you a new one.

中文翻譯

我確信我可以幫你。
不用擔心。
我會盡力。

我們會負起全部的責任。
我們的產品都是高品質的。
但是偶爾會有問題。

如果它壞了，你可以退貨。
我們不會問你任何問題。
我們會立刻更換。

有收據會讓事情更簡單。
它是個重要文件。
下一次，要把它放在安全的地方。

我不能退現金給你。
那樣你需要收據。
但我們保證會讓你滿意。

只要把那台烤麵包機帶回來店裡。
我們會回收。
我們會給你一台新的。

** ————————————————

responsibility〔rɪ,spɑnsə'bɪlətɪ〕*n.* 責任
occasionally〔ə'keʒənḷɪ〕*adv.* 偶爾
broken〔'brokən〕*adj.* 故障的　　replace〔rɪ'ples〕*v.* 更換
right away 立刻　　document〔'dɑkjəmənt〕*n.* 文件
refund〔'ri,fʌnd〕*n.* 退錢　　***make sure*** 確定
happy〔'hæpɪ〕*adj.* 滿意的　　***take back*** 將（退還之物）收下

Question 11: Express an Opinion

Track 02

Directions: In this part of the test, you will give your opinion about a specific topic. Be sure to say as much as you can in the time allowed. You will have 15 seconds to prepare. Then you will have 60 seconds to speak.

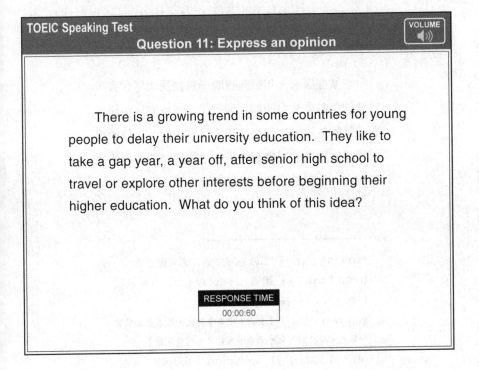

TOEIC Speaking Test
Question 11: Express an opinion
VOLUME

There is a growing trend in some countries for young people to delay their university education. They like to take a gap year, a year off, after senior high school to travel or explore other interests before beginning their higher education. What do you think of this idea?

RESPONSE TIME
00:00:60

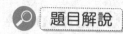 題目解說

> There is a growing trend in some countries for young people to delay their university education. They like to take a gap year, a year off, after senior high school to travel or explore other interests before beginning their higher education. What do you think of this idea?

在某些國家，年輕人會晚一點接受大學教育，這樣的趨勢愈來愈明顯。他們想要在唸完高中後，有一年的空檔，也就是一年的休息時間，來旅遊或探索其他讓他們感興趣的事，之後再開始他們的大學教育。你認為這個想法怎麼樣？

** ————————————————

growing (ˈgroɪŋ) adj. 在增加的；愈來愈強的

trend (trɛnd) n. 趨勢　　delay (dɪˈle) v. 延緩

take (tek) v. 採取

gap year 空檔年【意指高中畢業之後，還未上大學前，休息一段時間，到外面旅遊或打工，增廣見聞】

off (ɔf) adv. 休假　　explore (ɪkˈsplor) v. 探索

interest (ˈɪntrɪst) n. 感興趣的事

higher education 高等教育

必背答題範例   (Track 03)

I think it's good for some people.
They don't know what they want to do.
They need to experience life.

A gap year gives them time to think.
They can explore different careers.
They can find out what they're good at.

They can also use the time to travel.
They can discover other cultures.
They can broaden their horizons.

Some folks think it's a waste of time.
These kids are just playing around.
Maybe they will never go back to school.

I don't agree with that.
I think they'll come back.
And they'll be more mature.

They'll appreciate college more.
They will be more committed to it.
They will be better for the experience.

中文翻譯

我認為對某些人來說這是好的。
他們不知道他們想要做什麼。
他們需要去體驗人生。

一年的空檔給了他們時間去思考。
他們可以探索不同的職業。
他們可以了解他們擅長的是什麼。

他們也可以用這段時間去旅行。
他們可以發現其他的文化。
他們可以拓展自己的眼界。

有些人認為這是浪費時間。
這些孩子只是在四處遊蕩。
也許他們永遠不會回到學校。

我不同意那種看法。
我認為他們會回去。
而且他們會變得更成熟。

他們會更珍惜大學生活。
他們會更用心。
他們會因為這樣的經驗而變得更好。

**

experience〔ɪkˈspɪrɪəns〕*v.* 體驗 *n.* 經驗
career〔kəˈrɪr〕*n.* 職業　　discover〔dɪˈskʌvɚ〕*v.* 發現
culture〔ˈkʌltʃɚ〕*n.* 文化　　broaden〔ˈbrɔdn̩〕*v.* 拓展
horizons〔həˈraɪzn̩z〕*n. pl.* 眼界；知識範圍
folks〔foks〕*n. pl.* 人　　waste〔west〕*n.* 浪費
play around 四處遊蕩　　mature〔məˈtʃʊr〕*adj.* 成熟的
appreciate〔əˈprɪʃˌet〕*v.* 珍視　　***be committed to*** 致力於

TOEIC Speaking Test ②

Question 1: Read a Text Aloud

⊙ Track 04

Directions: In this part of the test, you will read aloud the text on the screen. You will have 45 seconds to prepare. Then you will have 45 seconds to read the text aloud.

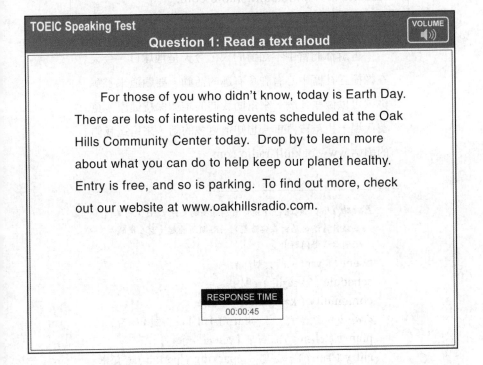

TOEIC Speaking Test

Question 1: Read a text aloud

VOLUME

For those of you who didn't know, today is Earth Day. There are lots of interesting events scheduled at the Oak Hills Community Center today. Drop by to learn more about what you can do to help keep our planet healthy. Entry is free, and so is parking. To find out more, check out our website at www.oakhillsradio.com.

RESPONSE TIME
00:00:45

題目解說 (Track 05)

> For those of you who didn't know, today is Earth Day. There are lots of interesting events scheduled at the Oak Hills Community Center today. Drop by to learn more about what you can do to help keep our planet healthy. Entry is free, and so is parking. To find out more, check out our website at www.oakhillsradio.com.

告訴你們當中不知道的人，今天是地球日。今天在橡樹丘社區中心有許多有趣的活動。要順道來了解你還可以做些什麼，來幫助我們的地球保持健康。免費入場，也免費停車。想知道更多的話，來逛逛我們的網站 www.oakhillsradio.com。

**

Earth Day 地球日【地球日為每年的 4 月 22 日，由美國參議員蓋洛‧尼爾森與丹尼斯‧海斯所發起，意在提醒人們關心環保問題】

event〔ɪˋvɛnt〕*n.* 大型活動

schedule〔ˋskɛdʒul〕*v.* 安排

community〔kəˋmjunətɪ〕*n.* 社區

drop by 順道拜訪   learn〔lɜn〕*v.* 得知；學習

planet〔ˋplænɪt〕*n.* 行星【在此指「地球」】

entry〔ˋɛntrɪ〕*n.* 入場   parking〔ˋparkɪŋ〕*n.* 停車

check out 看看   website〔ˋwɛb͵saɪt〕*n.* 網站

Question 2 : Read a Text Aloud

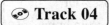 **Track 04**

Directions: In this part of the test, you will read aloud the text on the screen. You will have 45 seconds to prepare. Then you will have 45 seconds to read the text aloud.

TOEIC Speaking Test
Question 2: Read a text aloud

VOLUME

Have you ever dreamed about being the boss? Or perhaps you'd just like the freedom of working from home and setting your own hours. Marcy Cosmetics can help you achieve that. When you represent Marcy, you decide when and how much to work. You're the boss. And working with Marcy Cosmetics is fun, too. Simply invite your friends over for one of our cosmetics parties and earn a commission on every purchase they make. You'll not only have the fun of planning and participating in the party, but also be on your way to financial independence.

RESPONSE TIME
00:00:45

🔍 **題目解說** (🔊 **Track 05**)

> Have you ever dreamed about being the boss? Or perhaps you'd just like the freedom of working from home and setting your own hours. Marcy Cosmetics can help you achieve that. When you represent Marcy, you decide when and how much to work. You're the boss. And working with Marcy Cosmetics is fun, too. Simply invite your friends over for one of our cosmetics parties and earn a commission on every purchase they make. You'll not only have the fun of planning and participating in the party, but also be on your way to financial independence.

　　你曾經夢想過當老闆嗎？或者也許你只是想在家自由地工作，並且安排自己的時間。瑪茜化妝品可以幫你實現夢想。在你成為瑪茜的代表後，由你來決定工作時間和工作量。你就是老闆。在瑪茜化妝品工作也相當有趣。只要邀請你的朋友，來參加我們其中一個化妝品聚會，就可以從他們購買的每樣東西中獲得佣金。你不僅能從計劃和參加聚會中獲得快樂，還能朝著經濟獨立的目標邁進。

** ────────────

cosmetics〔kɑz'mɛtɪks〕 *n. pl.* 化粧品
achieve〔ə'tʃiv〕 *v.* 實現　　represent〔,rɛprɪ'zɛnt〕 *v.* 代表
invite sb. over 邀請某人過來
party〔'pɑrtɪ〕 *n.* 聚會【在此指直銷人員於家中所舉辦的聚會，在聚
　　會中向客戶介紹產品並接受訂單，也稱作 home party（家庭聚會）】
commission〔kə'mɪʃən〕 *n.* 佣金　　purchase〔'pɝtʃəs〕 *n.* 購買
participate〔pɑr'tɪsə,pet〕 *v.* 參與 < *in* >
financial〔fə'nænʃəl〕 *adj.* 財務的

Question 3 : Describe a Picture

🎧 Track 04

Directions: In this part of the test, you will describe the picture on your screen in as much detail as you can. You will have 30 seconds to prepare your response. Then you will have 45 seconds to speak about the picture.

必背答題範例 （ Track 05 ）

This is a food stand.
It's selling Greek food.
It's quite large.

The specialty is gyros.
That's a kind of sandwich.
It's made with bread and meat.

There are other things, too.
There are signs for grilled sausage and
  seafood milano.
They also sell strawberry and banana smoothies.

The stand is in front of a big building.
There are some people walking in front of it.
One is a woman with short hair.

It's a clear and sunny day.
The sun is shining on the roof of the stand.
It looks like striped canvas.

It's not too crowded.
Maybe it's early in the day.
I'm sure it will be popular later.

中文翻譯

這是一個賣食物的攤子。
它賣希臘料理。
它很大。

招牌菜是希臘式沙威瑪。
那是一種三明治。
以麵包和肉製成。

還有其他東西。
那裡有烤香腸和海鮮餅乾的招牌。
他們也賣草莓和香蕉口味的水果冰砂。

攤販位於一棟大樓的前方。
有一些人在它前面走動。
其中一位是個短髮的女士。

這是一個晴朗且陽光普照的日子。
陽光照耀在攤販的頂篷上。
它看起來像是有條紋的帆布。

這裡不會太擁擠。
可能是在一天中稍早的時候。
我確定晚一點會很熱鬧。

＊＊ ───────────────

stand〔stænd〕n. 攤子　　Greek〔grik〕adj. 希臘的
specialty〔'spɛʃəltɪ〕n. 招牌菜　　gyros〔'dʒaɪroz〕n. 希臘式沙威瑪
grilled〔grɪld〕adj. 烤的　　sausage〔'sɔsɪdʒ〕n. 香腸
milano〔mi'lɑno〕n. 餅乾的一種【milano 為義大利語的米蘭
　之意，此指源於義大利的一種餅乾】
smoothie〔'smuðɪ〕n. 加州式水果冰砂　　clear〔klɪr〕adj. 晴朗的
striped〔straɪpt〕adj. 有條紋的　　canvas〔'kænvəs〕n. 帆布

Questions 4-6 : Respond to Questions

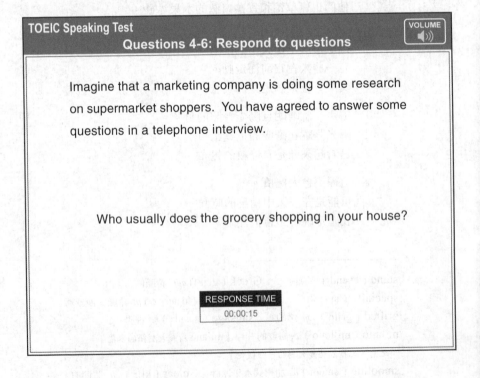

Track 04

Directions: In this part of the test, you will answer three questions. For each question, begin responding immediately after you hear a beep. No preparation time is provided. You will have 15 seconds to respond to Questions 4 and 5 and 30 seconds to respond to Question 6.

| TOEIC Speaking Test |
| VOLUME 🔊 |
| Questions 4-6: Respond to questions |

Imagine that a marketing company is doing some research on supermarket shoppers. You have agreed to answer some questions in a telephone interview.

Who usually does the grocery shopping in your house?

RESPONSE TIME
00:00:15

⇨ Question 5 is on the next page.

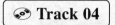

Track 04

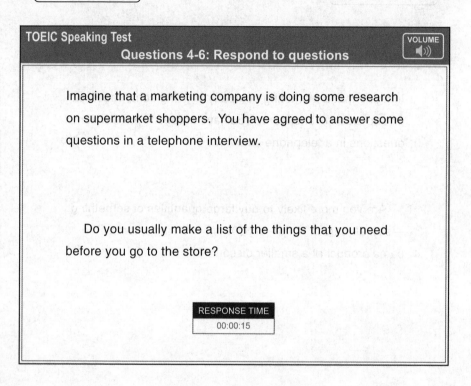

TOEIC Speaking Test
Questions 4-6: Respond to questions

VOLUME

Imagine that a marketing company is doing some research on supermarket shoppers. You have agreed to answer some questions in a telephone interview.

Do you usually make a list of the things that you need before you go to the store?

RESPONSE TIME
00:00:15

⇨ Question 6 is on the next page.

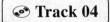

Track 04

TOEIC Speaking Test	VOLUME
Questions 4-6: Respond to questions	

Imagine that a marketing company is doing some research on supermarket shoppers. You have agreed to answer some questions in a telephone interview.

Are you more likely to buy large quantities of something —say, 20 bars of soap—at 30% off, or a single item of the same product at a smaller discount?

RESPONSE TIME
00:00:30

必背答題範例 （ Track 05 ）

Imagine that a marketing company is doing some research on supermarket shoppers. You have agreed to answer some questions in a telephone interview.

想像一下，有家行銷公司正在對超級市場的顧客進行調查。你已經同意在電話訪問中回答一些問題。

Q4: Who usually does the grocery shopping in your house?

在你家，通常是誰採買食品雜貨？

A4: I usually do the shopping. 我通常會去採購。
I do most of the cooking at our house.
我們家大多是由我掌廚。
So I know what to look for at the store.
所以我知道在店裡要找什麼東西。

Q5: Do you usually make a list of the things that you need before you go to the store?

在去商店之前，你通常會將你需要買的東西列成清單嗎？

A5: I always make a list. 我總是會列一張清單。
It helps me do the shopping faster.
這能幫我在採購時更迅速。
It also keeps me from forgetting anything.
這也能防止我忘記任何東西。

**

imagine〔ɪ'mædʒɪn〕*v.* 想像　　marketing〔'mɑrkɪtɪŋ〕*n.* 行銷
research〔'risɝtʃ〕*n.* 調查　　interview〔'ɪntɚˌvju〕*n.* 訪問
do the~shopping 購買~　　grocery〔'grosɚɪ〕*n.* 食品雜貨
make a list 列清單　　***keep sb. from~*** 防止某人~

Q6: Are you more likely to buy large quantities of something—say, 20 bars of soap—at 30% off, or a single item of the same product at a smaller discount?

你比較可能會大量購買某個商品——比如說，二十條肥皂——打七折，或是單買同樣的商品，但折扣較少？

A6: That depends on the product.
I don't have a lot of storage space.
So it has to be something I use a lot of.

I love getting big discounts.
Who doesn't?
But it's not a bargain if you can't use it.

Therefore, I tend to buy single items.
I'd rather save less than have to throw it away.
I don't like to waste things.

這要看是什麼產品。
我沒有很多儲藏的空間。
所以必須要是我使用量很大的東西。

我喜歡得到很大的折扣。
誰不喜歡呢？
但如果你買了卻用不到，那就不划算了。

因此，我傾向買單一商品。
我寧願少省一點錢，也不要將買來的東西丟掉。
我不喜歡浪費東西。

** ————————————————

quantity〔'kwɑntətɪ〕*n.* 數量　　say〔se〕*v.* 例如；比如說
bar〔bɑr〕*n.* 條　　***at 30% off*** 打七折
discount〔'dɪskaʊnt〕*n.* 折扣　　storage〔'storɪdʒ〕*n.* 儲藏
bargain〔'bɑrgɪn〕*n.* 划算的交易；便宜貨
tend to 傾向於　　***throw away*** 丟棄；浪費

Questions 7-9 : Respond to Questions Using Information Provided

Track 04

TOEIC Speaking Test

Questions 7-9: Respond to questions using information provided

 VOLUME

Directions: In this part of the test, you will answer three questions based on the information provided. You will have 30 seconds to read the information before the questions begin. For each question, begin responding immediately after you hear a beep. No additional preparation time is provided. You will have 15 seconds to respond to Questions 7 and 8 and 30 seconds to respond to Question 9.

Summer Camp

Where: Beverley Lake
When: August 1-10
Who: Kids 8 -12

This year's camp will be run by Les Watkins, director of the local YMCA. Activities include swimming, horseback riding, hiking, arts and crafts, and lessons in all kinds of outdoor skills.

➤ **To register :** Registration forms are available at the school office. Be sure to send yours in by July 15. Late registrations will not be accepted.

➤ **The cost :** Camp fee, $120
Transportation to Lake Beverley, $10
Bedding, if needed, $20

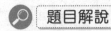

題目解說

【中文翻譯】

夏令營

地點：貝薇莉湖

時間：八月一日到十日

對象：八到十二歲兒童

今年的夏令營，是由當地的基督教青年會的主任萊斯‧華津所舉辦。活動包括游泳、騎馬、健行、手工藝，和各種戶外技能課程。

➤ **報名方式：**報名表可在學校辦公室索取。務必在七月十五日前送交報名表。逾期報名將不予受理。

➤ **費　　用：**露營費，120 美元

至貝薇莉湖的交通費，10 美元

如需寢具，20 美元

【背景敘述】

> Hi! This is Don Matthews. Our kids go to Simpson Elementary together. My son wants to go to the summer camp they've got, but I've lost the flyer. Can I ask you a few questions?

嗨！我是唐・馬修。我們的小孩都就讀辛普森小學。我兒子想去夏令營，但是我把傳單弄丟了。我可以問你一些問題嗎？

**

run〔rʌn〕v. 管理；舉辦
director〔dəˈrɛktɚ〕n. 主任
YMCA 基督教青年會（= Young Men's Christian
　Association）　　horseback〔ˈhɔrs,bæk〕n. 馬背
horseback riding 騎馬　　craft〔kræft〕n. 工藝
arts and crafts 手工藝
register〔ˈrɛdʒɪstɚ〕v. 註冊；報名

registration〔ˌrɛdʒɪˈstreʃən〕n. 報名
form〔fɔrm〕n. 表格
available〔əˈveləbḷ〕adj. 可獲得的
send in 遞送　　fee〔fi〕n. 費用
transportation〔ˌtrænspɚˈteʃən〕n. 交通費
bedding〔ˈbɛdɪŋ〕n. 寢具　　***have got*** 有
flyer〔ˈflaɪɚ〕n. 傳單

必背答題範例 (☺ **Track 05**)

Q7: Where is the camp going to be?

這個夏令營將在哪裡舉辦？

A7: It's at Lake Beverley.

That's a beautiful spot.

It's very clean and safe.

在貝薇莉湖。

那是個很美的地點。

非常乾淨而且安全。

Q8: What can the kids do there?

孩子們在那裡可以做什麼？

A8: There are all kinds of activities.

Most of them are outdoor things.

They've got hiking, riding, and swimming.

有各種的活動。

大部分是戶外活動。

他們有健行、騎馬和游泳。

**

spot〔spɑt〕*n.* 地點

Q9: Do you think it's worth sending the kids there?
你認為把小孩送去那裡值得嗎？

A9: I sure do.
I send my son every year.
It's a great chance for him to get outdoors.

It's not that expensive.
It's only $120.
That's a bargain if you ask me.

He really enjoys it.
He has a great time every year.
He's definitely going again this year.

我相信非常值得。
我每年都送我兒子去。
對他而言，這是一個接觸大自然的好機會。

它並沒有那麼昂貴。
只要一百二十美元。
如果你問我的話，我會說這很划算。

他非常喜歡這個夏令營。
他每年都玩得很愉快。
他今年一定會再去。

** ——————————————————

worth 〔wɜθ〕 *adj.* 值得的
have a great time 玩得很愉快
definitely 〔'dɛfənɪtlɪ〕 *adv.* 肯定地

Question 10 : Propose a Solution

⊛ Track 04

Directions: In this part of the test, you will be presented with a problem and asked to propose a solution. You will have 30 seconds to prepare. Then you will have 60 seconds to speak. In your response, be sure to show that you recognize the problem, and propose a way of dealing with the problem.

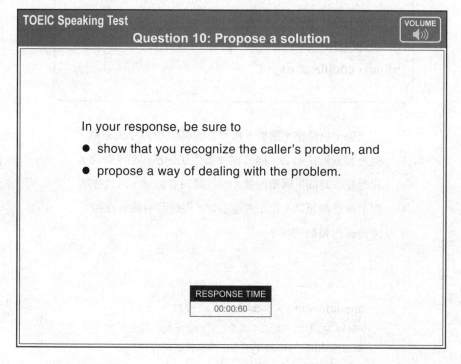

➡ Now listen to the voice message.

 題目解說

【語音留言】

> Hi. This is Lou Norton. I have an appointment with Dr. Garren today at 3:00, but I can't make it. Something has come up at the office. Anyway, I'd like to reschedule. The trouble is I'm going out of town on Thursday and will be gone for at least three weeks. I know she's busy, but is there any chance I can get an appointment within the next couple of days?

　　嗨，我是羅‧諾頓。我和嘉倫醫生預約今天三點，但是我沒辦法過去。辦公室裡發生了一些事情。總之，我想要改時間。麻煩的是，我星期四要出城，而且會離開至少三個星期。我知道她很忙，但是我有機會在接下來幾天內預約到嗎？

** ────────────────

appointment〔ə'pɔɪntmənt〕*n.* 預約
make it 辦到；能去；能來　　***come up*** 發生
reschedule〔ri'skɛdʒul〕*v.* 重新安排時間
couple〔'kʌpḷ〕*n.* 幾個

必背答題範例 (Track 05)

Thanks for calling, Mr. Norton.
I appreciate your canceling the appointment.
Thanks for letting us know.

I understand that you need to see the doctor
  soon.
I know that your time is limited to two days.
I'll see what I can do.

It would be best if you saw her before you leave.
I'll check if there are any openings.
If not, I'm sure I can find another way.

If you are flexible with your time, that will help.
You could come early in the morning.
Or she could see you in the evening.

Another option is a cancellation.
Someone else might not be able to make it.
You could take their spot.

I'll let you know the times that are available.
I'll call you back as soon as possible.
I'm sure we can work something out.

📄 中文翻譯

謝謝你的來電，諾頓先生。
感謝你來取消預約。
謝謝你通知我們。

我了解你必須儘早看醫生。
我知道你的時間只剩這兩天。
我會看看我能做些什麼。

如果你能在離開之前見到她是最好的。
我會查一下是否還有任何空檔時間。
如果沒有，我確信我能找到別的辦法。

如果你的時間有彈性的話，會有很大的幫助。
你可以早上早一點過來。
或者她可以在晚上與你見面。

另一個選擇是等別人取消。
其他人可能無法依約前來。
你可以補他們的缺。

我會告訴你可以來的時間。
我會盡快回電話給你。
我確信我們可以想出解決辦法。

** ─────────────────────

appreciate〔əˋpriʃɪ͵et〕v. 感激　　cancel〔ˋkænsl̩〕v. 取消
limit〔ˋlɪmɪt〕v. 限制　　opening〔ˋopənɪŋ〕n. 空缺
flexible〔ˋflɛksəbl̩〕adj. 有彈性的　　option〔ˋɑpʃən〕n. 選擇
cancellation〔͵kænsəˋleʃən〕n. 取消
spot〔spɑt〕n.（序列中的）位置　　***work out*** 解決；想出

Question 11 : Express an Opinion

 **Track 04**

Directions: In this part of the test, you will give your opinion about a specific topic. Be sure to say as much as you can in the time allowed. You will have 15 seconds to prepare. Then you will have 60 seconds to speak.

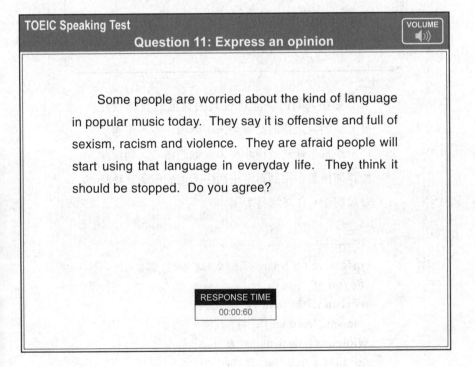

TOEIC Speaking Test
Question 11: Express an opinion
VOLUME

Some people are worried about the kind of language in popular music today. They say it is offensive and full of sexism, racism and violence. They are afraid people will start using that language in everyday life. They think it should be stopped. Do you agree?

RESPONSE TIME
00:00:60

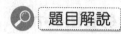 題目解說

> Some people are worried about the kind of language in popular music today. They say it is offensive and full of sexism, racism and violence. They are afraid people will start using that language in everyday life. They think it should be stopped. Do you agree?

有些人對時下流行音樂的那種語言感到擔憂。他們說這樣的語言令人不舒服,並且充滿了性別歧視、種族歧視和暴力。他們擔心人們會開始將那種語言用到日常生活中。他們認為它應該要被制止。你同意嗎?

**

offensive〔ə'fɛnsɪv〕*adj.* 令人不快的;觸怒人的
be full of 充滿了
sexism〔'sɛks,ɪzəm〕*n.* 性別歧視
racism〔'resɪzəm〕*n.* 種族歧視
violence〔'vaɪələns〕*n.* 暴力
afraid〔ə'fred〕*adj.* 擔心的
everyday〔'ɛvrɪ'de〕*adj.* 每天的;日常的
stop〔stɑp〕*v.* 阻止

必背答題範例 (Track 05)

I agree that there is a lot of offensive language.
But it's not just in music.
You also hear it in movies and on TV.

I don't think we can stop it, though.
That would be censorship.
The singers should have freedom of speech.

Language changes over time.
It's impossible to control.
It's a natural process.

But I do think we can do something about it.
We can refuse to buy albums that offend us.
When their sales drop, the artists will get
    the message.

Parents can help, too.
They should know what their kids are
    listening to.
They can talk to them about it.

In the end, it's up to us.
No one can put words in our mouths.
We are the ones who decide what we say.

中文翻譯

我同意有許多令人不舒服的語言。
但不只在音樂中。
你也可以在電影和電視上聽到。

然而,我不認為我們能制止。
那會變成審查制度。
歌手該有言論的自由。

語言會隨著時間而改變。
要控制它是不可能的。
這是個自然的過程。

但是我的確認為我們可以做些什麼。
我們可以拒買那些令我們感到不舒服的專輯。
當他們的銷售量下降,這些藝人就會明白了。

父母也可以幫上忙。
他們應該要知道他們的小孩在聽些什麼。
他們可以和小孩談論這件事。

這終究是由我們自己決定。
沒有人可以教我們怎麼說。
我們才是決定自己要說什麼話的人。

** ────────────────────────

though〔ðo〕*adv.*【置於句尾】不過
censorship〔'sɛnsə‚ʃɪp〕*n.* 審查制度
freedom〔'fridəm〕*n.* 自由　　*over time* 隨著時間
album〔'ælbəm〕*n.* 專輯　　*offend*〔ə'fɛnd〕*v.* 使不舒服
artist〔'artɪst〕*n.* 藝人　　*get the message* 了解含意
in the end 最後;終究　　*be up to sb.* 由某人決定
put words in one's mouth 敎某人怎麼說

TOEIC Speaking Test ③

Question 1: Read a Text Aloud

 **Track 06**

Directions: In this part of the test, you will read aloud the text on the screen. You will have 45 seconds to prepare. Then you will have 45 seconds to read the text aloud.

TOEIC Speaking Test

VOLUME 🔊

Question 1: Read a text aloud

The downtown Sherling Hotel is offering a weekend getaway package for two. The package includes a junior suite for Friday and Saturday night, breakfast, complimentary theater tickets and late checkout on Sunday. This is a great opportunity to discover what the city has to offer while enjoying the comforts of a first-class hotel.

RESPONSE TIME
00:00:45

題目解說 (✎ **Track 07**)

The downtown Sherling Hotel is offering a weekend getaway package for two. The package includes a junior suite for Friday and Saturday night, breakfast, complimentary theater tickets and late checkout on Sunday. This is a great opportunity to discover what the city has to offer while enjoying the comforts of a first-class hotel.

市中心的謝林飯店，正推出兩人成行的週末渡假套裝行程。行程包括星期五和星期六晚上的簡單套房、早餐、免費的電影票，以及星期天延後退房。這是個探索這個城市的大好機會，同時又能享受一流飯店裡舒適的設備。

** ─────────

offer〔ˋɔfɚ〕v. 提供　　getaway〔ˋgɛtəˌwe〕n. 逃走；出發
package〔ˋpækɪdʒ〕n. 套裝商品
getaway package 渡假套裝行程
junior〔ˋdʒunjɚ〕adj. 地位較低的　　suite〔swit〕n. 套房
junior suite 簡單套房；商旅套房
complimentary〔ˌkɑmpləˋmɛntərɪ〕adj. 免費的；贈送的
checkout〔ˋtʃɛkˌaʊt〕n. 結帳退房
comforts〔ˋkʌmfɚts〕n. pl. 使生活舒服的東西
first-class〔ˋfɝstˋklæs〕adj. 一流的；上等的

Question 2 : Read a Text Aloud

 **Track 06**

Directions: In this part of the test, you will read aloud the text on the screen. You will have 45 seconds to prepare. Then you will have 45 seconds to read the text aloud.

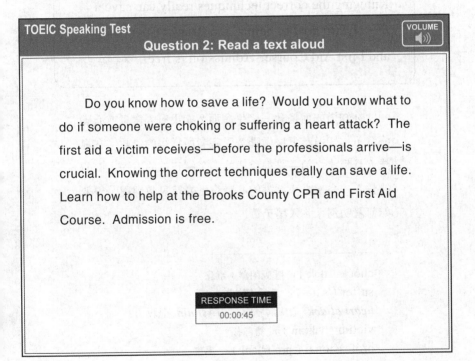

TOEIC Speaking Test

Question 2: Read a text aloud

VOLUME

Do you know how to save a life? Would you know what to do if someone were choking or suffering a heart attack? The first aid a victim receives—before the professionals arrive—is crucial. Knowing the correct techniques really can save a life. Learn how to help at the Brooks County CPR and First Aid Course. Admission is free.

RESPONSE TIME
00:00:45

題目解說 (**Track 07**)

Do you know how to save a life? Would you know what to do if someone were choking or suffering a heart attack? The first aid a victim receives—before the professionals arrive—is crucial. Knowing the correct techniques really can save a life. Learn how to help at the Brooks County CPR and First Aid Course. Admission is free.

你知道如何挽救一條生命嗎？如果有人窒息或心臟病發，你知道該怎麼做嗎？受害者所獲得的急救——在專業人員到達之前——是很重要的。了解正確的方法，真的能救人一命。來小溪郡的心肺復甦術及急救課程，學習如何幫助別人。入場免費。

**

chock〔tʃɔk〕*v.* 呼吸困難；窒息
suffer〔'sʌfə〕*v.* 遭受（痛苦）
heart attack 心臟病發作　　***first aid*** 急救
victim〔'vɪktɪm〕*n.* 受害者
professional〔prə'fɛʃən̩〕*n.* 專家
crucial〔'kruʃəl〕*adj.* 非常重要的
technique〔tɛk'nik〕*n.* 方法；技巧
CPR 心肺復甦術（= *cardiopulmonary resuscitation*）
admission〔əd'mɪʃən〕*n.* 入場（許可）

Question 3 : Describe a Picture

Track 06

Directions: In this part of the test, you will describe the picture on your screen in as much detail as you can. You will have 30 seconds to prepare your response. Then you will have 45 seconds to speak about the picture.

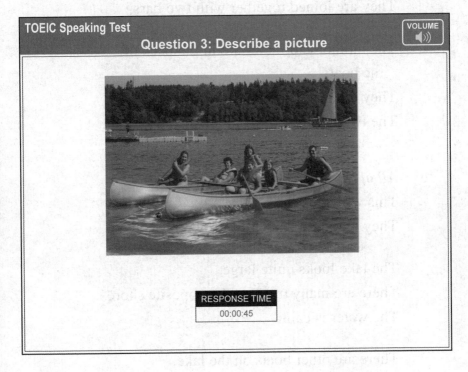

TOEIC Speaking Test

Question 3: Describe a picture

VOLUME

RESPONSE TIME
00:00:45

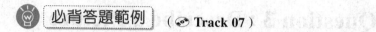

必背答題範例 (Track 07)

Some people are out on a lake.
I think they are a family.
There are a mother, father and four kids.

The family has two boats.
They are canoes.
They are joined together with two bars.

The mother and father are in the back of
   the boats.
They are paddling.
The two children in front are also paddling.

All of them are wearing life vests.
This will keep them safe.
They are in no danger of drowning.

The lake looks quite large.
There are many trees on the opposite shore.
The water is calm.

There are other boats on the lake.
One is a sailboat.
Another is a small motorboat.

中文翻譯

有些人在湖面上。
我想他們是一家人。
有媽媽、爸爸，和四個小孩。

這家人有兩條船。
它們是獨木舟。
它們用兩根棍子連在一起。

媽媽和爸爸在船的後面。
他們正在划船。
在前面的兩個小孩也在划船。

他們全都穿著救生衣。
這能使他們安全。
他們不會有溺水的危險。

湖看起來相當大。
對岸有很多樹。
水面很平靜。

湖上也有其他的船。
有一艘是帆船。
另一艘是小型汽艇。

** ───────────────────

out〔aʊt〕*adv.*（船等）離開陸地；出海
canoe〔kə'nu〕*n.* 獨木舟　　bar〔bɑr〕*n.* 棍子
paddle〔'pædl〕*v.* 用槳划船　*in front* 在前面（*= ahead*）
life vest 救生衣　　*in danger of* 處於…危險之中
drown〔draʊn〕*v.* 溺水　　opposite〔'ɑpəzɪt〕*adj.* 對面的
shore〔ʃor〕*n.*（湖）岸　　sailboat〔'sel,bot〕*n.* 帆船
motorboat〔'motɚ,bot〕*n.* 汽艇

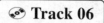
Questions 4-6 : Respond to Questions

** Track 06**

Directions: In this part of the test, you will answer three questions. For each question, begin responding immediately after you hear a beep. No preparation time is provided. You will have 15 seconds to respond to Questions 4 and 5 and 30 seconds to respond to Question 6.

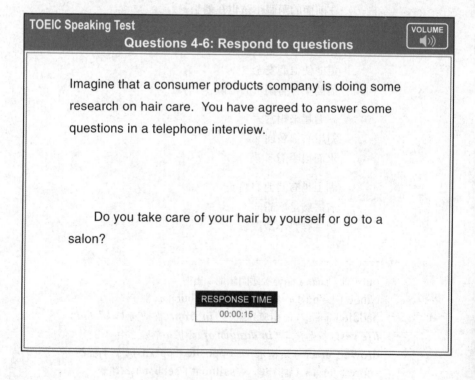

TOEIC Speaking Test
Questions 4-6: Respond to questions
VOLUME

Imagine that a consumer products company is doing some research on hair care. You have agreed to answer some questions in a telephone interview.

Do you take care of your hair by yourself or go to a salon?

RESPONSE TIME
00:00:15

⇨ Question 5 is on the next page.

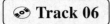 **Track 06**

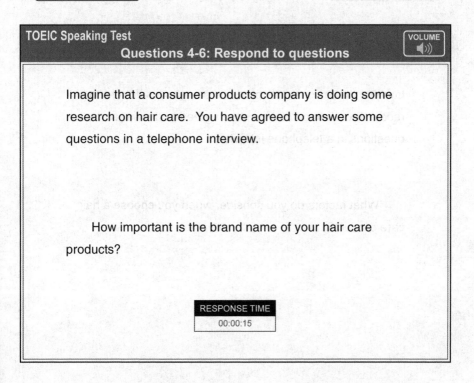

TOEIC Speaking Test
Questions 4-6: Respond to questions

VOLUME

Imagine that a consumer products company is doing some research on hair care. You have agreed to answer some questions in a telephone interview.

How important is the brand name of your hair care products?

RESPONSE TIME
00:00:15

⇨ Question 6 is on the next page.

 Track 06

TOEIC Speaking Test
VOLUME
◀))
Questions 4-6: Respond to questions

Imagine that a consumer products company is doing some research on hair care. You have agreed to answer some questions in a telephone interview.

What factors do you consider when you choose a hair care product?

RESPONSE TIME
00:00:30

必背答題範例 （ ◈ **Track 07** ）

Imagine that a consumer products company is doing some research on hair care. You have agreed to answer some questions in a telephone interview.

想像一下，有家消費者商品公司正在進行有關護髮的調查。你已同意於電話訪問中回答一些問題。

Q4： Do you take care of your hair by yourself or go to a salon?
你都自己整理頭髮還是去美容院？

A4： I usually take care of my hair by myself.
我通常自己整理頭髮。
I go to a salon every few weeks.
我每隔幾週去一次美容院。
I usually get my hair cut then.
我通常都在那時剪頭髮。

Q5： How important is the brand name of your hair care products?
護髮產品的品牌對你有多重要？

A5： Brand name is pretty important. 品牌是相當重要的。
I trust certain brands. 我相信某些品牌。
But I also listen to my friends' opinions.
但我也會聽聽朋友們的意見。

** ————————————

consumer〔kən'sumɚ〕*n.* 消費者
consumer products company 消費者商品公司
take care of 照顧　　salon〔sɑ'lõ〕*n.* 美容院
brand name 品牌　　***hair care product*** 護髮產品
certain〔'sɝtn̩〕*adj.* 某些

Q6: What factors do you consider when you choose
a hair care product?

選擇護髮產品時，你會考量哪些因素？

A6: Well, first I think about quality.
I want a product that works.
I want my hair to look good.

Then I think about price.
I'm only willing to pay so much.
Some products are really overpriced.

And I guess I'm influenced by the package.
I prefer cute and stylish products.
But that's not as important as the first two things.

嗯，首先我會考慮品質。
我要有效的產品。
我希望我的頭髮看起來很棒。

再來我會考慮價格。
我只願意付出一定的錢。
有些產品的定價實在太高了。

接著我想我會受包裝影響。
我比較喜歡可愛和時髦的產品。
但是那沒有像前兩項那麼重要。

** ────────────────────

quality〔'kwɑlətɪ〕*n.* 品質　　work〔wɜk〕*v.* 有效
willing〔'wɪlɪŋ〕*adj.* 願意的
overpriced〔ˌovə'praɪst〕*adj.* 定價過高的
influence〔'ɪnfluəns〕*v.* 影響　　package〔'pækɪdʒ〕*n.* 包裝
prefer〔prɪ'fɜ〕*v.* 比較喜歡　　stylish〔'staɪlɪʃ〕*adj.* 時髦的

Questions 7-9 : Respond to Questions Using Information Provided

Track 06

TOEIC Speaking Test
Questions 7-9: Respond to questions using information provided

VOLUME

Directions: In this part of the test, you will answer three questions based on the information provided. You will have 30 seconds to read the information before the questions begin. For each question, begin responding immediately after you hear a beep. No additional preparation time is provided. You will have 15 seconds to respond to Questions 7 and 8 and 30 seconds to respond to Question 9.

Brooks County Fair

Where: County Fairground, Highway 19 near Applewood

When: Saturday, July 17, 8 a.m.-11 p.m.

What: ∗ Giant Ferris Wheel and other great rides

∗ the Brooks Senior High School marching band

∗ ring toss, shooting gallery and more games

∗ livestock show and awards

∗ farm produce show and awards

∗ lots of great food and family fun!

Cost: Adult Admission $6

Children under 12 $4

Children under 3 Free

Entry for livestock or produce contest: $3

題目解說

【中文翻譯】

小溪郡農產品大賽

地　　點：郡立評審會場，蘋果森林附近的 19 號公路

時　　間：7 月 17 日，星期六，早上 8 點至晚上 11 點

內　　容：＊大型摩天輪及其他頂級遊樂設施

　　　　　＊小溪高中軍樂隊

　　　　　＊套圈圈、打靶及更多遊戲

　　　　　＊家畜展示及評比

　　　　　＊農產品展示及評比

　　　　　＊大量的美食和家庭娛樂！

費　　用：成人入場費　6 美元

　　　　　12 歲以下兒童　4 美元

　　　　　3 歲以下兒童　免費

　　　　　參加畜產或農產比賽：　3 美元

【背景敘述】

> Hello.　I'm trying to find out about the county fair.　Could I ask you a few questions about it?

哈囉。我想了解小溪郡農產品大賽的資訊。我能問你一些相關的問題嗎？

＊＊ ────────────

fair〔fɛr〕*n.*（農產品、畜產品的）品評會；賽會

fairground〔'fɛr,graʊnd〕*n.* 評審會場

highway〔'haɪ,we〕*n.* 公路

giant〔'dʒaɪənt〕*adj.* 巨大的

Ferris wheel 摩天輪

ride〔raɪd〕*n.*（遊樂場的）乘坐物

marching band 軍樂隊

ring toss 套圈圈　　***shooting gallery*** 打靶場

livestock〔'laɪv,stɑk〕*n.* 家畜

show〔ʃo〕*n.* 展示

award〔ə'wɔrd〕*n.* 判決；裁定

produce〔'prɑdjus〕*n. pl.* 農產品

adult〔ə'dʌlt〕*n.* 成人

admission〔əd'mɪʃən〕*n.* 入場（費）

entry〔'ɛntrɪ〕*n.* 加入　　contest〔'kɑntɛst〕*n.* 比賽

必背答題範例   (☉ **Track 07**)

Q7: Where and when is it going to be?

請問農產品大賽將於何處及何時舉辦呢？

A7: It's going to be at the fairground.

That's near Applewood.

It's on Saturday, July 17th.

它將在評審會場舉行。

那裡接近蘋果森林。

在七月十七日星期六舉行。

Q8: How much does it cost?

它要花多少錢呢？

A8: It's six dollars for adults.

Kids pay four, and children under three are
free.

There's an extra fee if you enter something in
a contest.

成人要六美元。

小孩要付四美元，而三歲以下小孩免費。

如果你要參加競賽的話，要多付額外的費用。

** ——————————————————

pay〔pe〕*v.* 支付　　extra〔'ɛkstrə〕*adj.* 額外的

fee〔fi〕*n.* 費用　　enter〔'ɛntɚ〕*v.* 使…參加比賽

Q9: What kind of things can we do there?
　　我們能在那裡做些什麼事？

A9: There will be lots of rides and games.
　　The giant Ferris wheel is the most popular.
　　You can also try your luck at the ring toss.

　　You can look at the farm animals.
　　Farmers will show off their cows or pigs.
　　They can win prizes for the best one.

　　And then there is always some great food.
　　There will be music, too.
　　The high school band is going to perform.

　　那裡會有很多的遊樂設施及遊戲。
　　大型摩天輪是最受歡迎的。
　　你也可以玩套圈圈試試你的運氣。

　　你可以參觀農場的動物。
　　農夫們將會展示他們的乳牛或豬。
　　最好的那一隻可以得獎。

　　而且還會持續供應一些美食。
　　現場也會有音樂。
　　會有高中的樂隊來表演。

**　———————————————

popular〔'pɑpjələ〕adj. 受歡迎的
try one's luck 試試運氣
show off 炫耀；展現　　cow〔kaʊ〕n. 母牛
prize〔praɪz〕n. 獎　　perform〔pɚ'fɔrm〕v. 表演

Question 10 : Propose a Solution

Track 06

Directions: In this part of the test, you will be presented with a problem and asked to propose a solution. You will have 30 seconds to prepare. Then you will have 60 seconds to speak. In your response, be sure to show that you recognize the problem, and propose a way of dealing with the problem.

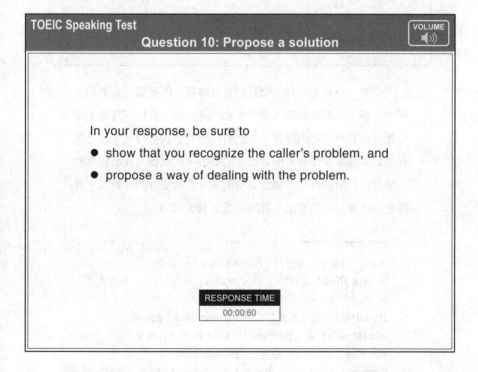

TOEIC Speaking Test
Question 10: Propose a solution
VOLUME

In your response, be sure to

● show that you recognize the caller's problem, and
● propose a way of dealing with the problem.

RESPONSE TIME
00:00:60

➡ Now listen to the voice message.

🔍 題目解說

【語音留言】

> Hello. I'm calling about booking a flight to Atlanta. I really need to go tomorrow, but I haven't been able to find any available seats. I'd prefer to fly business class, but at this point I'll take anything you have. I have to be there by 10:00 for a meeting, so I need to get on an early morning flight. I've heard your agency is really good at getting last minute seats. I hope you can help me out. My name is Todd Barkley and my number is 589-1256.

哈囉。我打來是為了預訂前往亞特蘭大的班機。我真的必須明天就走,但我到現在還找不到任何空位。我比較喜歡坐商務艙,但是現在這種時候,你們有什麼位子我都接受。我必須在十點前到那裡開會,所以我必須搭很早的班機。我聽說你們這家旅行社對於訂臨時機位很有辦法。我希望你們能幫我。我的名字是泰德‧巴克萊,我的電話是589-1256。

** ────────────────────

book〔buk〕v. 預訂　　flight〔flaɪt〕n. 班機
book a flight 預訂班機　　Atlanta〔ət'læntə〕n. 亞特蘭大
available〔ə'veləbḷ〕adj. 可獲得的
fly〔flaɪ〕v. 搭(飛機)　　**business class** 商務艙
at this point 在這個時間點　　take〔tek〕v. 接受
meeting〔'mitɪŋ〕n. 會議　　**get on** 搭乘
agency〔'edʒənsɪ〕n. 代辦處【在此指 travel agency(旅行社)】
last minute 臨時的;及時的　　**help sb. out** 幫忙某人

 必背答題範例 (Track 07)

Mr. Barkley, this is Jane from Sun Travel.
I got your message and I've looked into the
  flights to Atlanta.
I understand that you need to arrive by 10 a.m.

All of the morning flights are fully booked.
That includes both business and economy class.
So I can't get you a reserved seat.

You have some options, though.
There are things that you can do.
Let me explain them to you.

First, I could put you on standby.
If someone misses the plane, you can get a seat.
But there's a risk that you won't get on.

Another option is to take the 9 a.m. flight.
There are seats available.
It arrives at 10:30.

Or you could fly there tonight.
There's a flight at 9 p.m.
Please think about it and call me back.

中文翻譯

巴克萊先生，我是陽光旅行社的珍。
我聽到了你的留言，並且我查過往亞特蘭大的班機。
我知道你必須在早上十點之前到達。

早上的班機全部都被訂滿了。
包括商務艙和經濟艙。
所以我無法給你預訂的座位。

不過，你還是有些選擇。
你還是能做點別的事。
讓我解釋給你聽。

首先，我可以幫你排候補。
如果有人錯過班機，你就會有位子。
但是你有搭不到飛機的風險。

另一個選擇是搭乘早上九點的班機。
它還有空位。
它會在十點半到達。

或者你可以今晚就搭飛機去那裡。
有一班晚上九點的班機。
請你考慮一下然後回電給我。

** ——————————————————

message〔ˋmɛsɪdʒ〕 *n.* 訊息；留言　　 ***look into*** 調查
economy class 經濟艙　　 reserved〔rɪˋzɝvd〕 *adj.* 預訂的
option〔ˋɑpʃən〕 *n.* 選擇　　 though〔ðo〕 *adv.*【置於句尾】不過
put〔put〕 *v.* 使處於（某種狀態）
on standby 等待著（別人的退票以便補上）
risk〔rɪsk〕 *n.* 風險　　 ***call sb. back*** 回某人電話

Question 11 : Express an Opinion

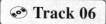 **Track 06**

Directions: In this part of the test, you will give your opinion about a specific topic. Be sure to say as much as you can in the time allowed. You will have 15 seconds to prepare. Then you will have 60 seconds to speak.

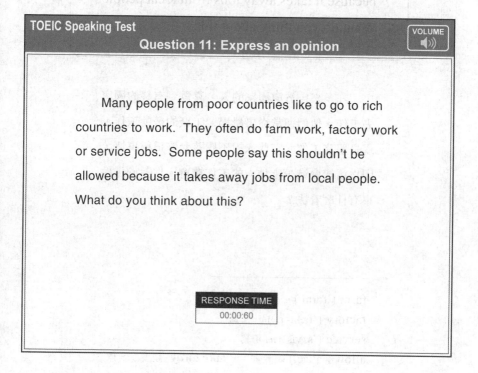

TOEIC Speaking Test

Question 11: Express an opinion

VOLUME

Many people from poor countries like to go to rich countries to work. They often do farm work, factory work or service jobs. Some people say this shouldn't be allowed because it takes away jobs from local people. What do you think about this?

RESPONSE TIME
00:00:60

題目解說

> 　　Many people from poor countries like
> to go to rich countries to work. They often
> do farm work, factory work or service jobs.
> Some people say this shouldn't be allowed
> because it takes away jobs from local people.
> What do you think about this?

　　許多來自貧窮國家的人，喜歡到有錢的國家去工作。他們通常從事農場、工廠的勞動工作，或是服務工作。有些人說不應該允許這種事情，因為這樣會減少當地人的工作機會。你對於這件事有什麼看法？

** ————————

farm〔farm〕n. 農場
factory〔'fæktərɪ〕n. 工廠
service〔'sɜvɪs〕n. 服務
allow〔ə'lau〕v. 允許　　　*take away* 減去；剝奪
local〔'lokḷ〕adj. 當地的

必背答題範例 (Track 07)

In my opinion, rich countries need foreign workers.
They do the jobs other people don't want to do.
And they do them for a lot less money.

Employers need foreign workers.
Without them, they might not be able to fill jobs.
They might have to close their businesses.

If they hired local people, they'd have to pay more.
That would raise the price of the goods.
Everyone would pay more in the end.

Some people think foreign workers hurt their economy.
I don't agree.
I think they help it.

Without them, the economy could not grow.
Developed countries have low birth rates.
There aren't enough young workers.

The factories and jobs might move elsewhere.
Then the government would lose taxes.
Without foreign workers, everyone loses.

中文翻譯

我認為有錢的國家需要外籍勞工。
他們做那些其他人不想做的工作。
而且他們拿的薪水少很多。

雇主們需要外籍勞工。
沒有他們，雇主可能無法填滿職缺。
他們可能必須關門大吉。

如果雇主雇用當地人，他們得付更多的錢。
那樣會提高商品的價格。
最後，每個人都將付更多的錢。

有些人認為外籍勞工危害了他們的經濟。
我不同意。
我認為他們有助於經濟。

沒有外籍勞工，經濟可能不會成長。
已開發國家的出生率低。
它們沒有足夠的年輕勞工。

工廠和工作機會可能移到別的地方。
然後政府會失去稅收。
沒有了外籍勞工，大家都會損失。

**

foreign worker 外籍勞工　　**employer** (ɪmˋplɔɪɚ) *n.* 雇主
fill (fɪl) *v.* 填滿（空缺）　　**business** (ˋbɪznɪs) *n.* 公司；企業
goods (gudz) *n. pl.* 商品　　**economy** (ɪˋkɑnəmɪ) *n.* 經濟
developed country 已開發國家　　***birth rate*** 出生率
move (muv) *v.* 遷移　　**elsewhere** (ˋɛls,hwɛr) *adv.* 到別處
government (ˋgʌvɚmənt) *n.* 政府
lose (luz) *v.* 失去；蒙受損失　　**tax** (tæks) *n.* 稅

TOEIC Speaking Test ④

Question 1: Read a Text Aloud

☺ Track 08

Directions: In this part of the test, you will read aloud the text on the screen. You will have 45 seconds to prepare. Then you will have 45 seconds to read the text aloud.

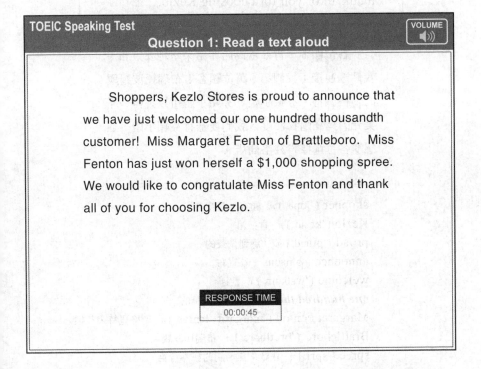

TOEIC Speaking Test
Question 1: Read a text aloud

VOLUME

Shoppers, Kezlo Stores is proud to announce that we have just welcomed our one hundred thousandth customer! Miss Margaret Fenton of Brattleboro. Miss Fenton has just won herself a $1,000 shopping spree. We would like to congratulate Miss Fenton and thank all of you for choosing Kezlo.

RESPONSE TIME
00:00:45

題目解說 (Track 09)

> Shoppers, Kezlo Stores is proud to announce that we have just welcomed our one hundred thousandth customer! Miss Margaret Fenton of Brattleboro. Miss Fenton has just won herself a $1,000 shopping spree. We would like to congratulate Miss Fenton and thank all of you for choosing Kezlo.

各位顧客，肯茲洛商店非常榮幸地要宣布，我們剛迎接了我們第十萬位顧客！布瑞托波羅鎮的瑪格麗特‧芬頓小姐。芬頓小姐可以獲得一千美元的瘋狂購物額度。我們要恭喜芬頓小姐，並感謝各位選擇肯茲洛商店。

** ————————————————

shopper〔ˈʃɑpɚ〕n. 顧客；購物者
Kezlo〔ˈkɛzlo〕n. 肯茲洛
proud〔praʊd〕adj. 感到光榮的
announce〔əˈnaʊns〕v. 宣布
welcome〔ˈwɛlkəm〕v. 歡迎
one hundred thousandth 第十萬的
Margaret Fenton〔ˈmɑrgərɪt ˈfɛntən〕n. 瑪格麗特‧芬頓
Brattleboro〔ˈbrætl̩bərə〕n. 布瑞托波羅
spree〔spri〕n. 狂歡；無節制的狂熱行為
congratulate〔kənˈgrætʃəˌlet〕v. 祝賀；恭喜

Question 2 : Read a Text Aloud

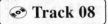 **Track 08**

Directions: In this part of the test, you will read aloud the text on the screen. You will have 45 seconds to prepare. Then you will have 45 seconds to read the text aloud.

TOEIC Speaking Test | VOLUME 🔊
Question 2: Read a text aloud

It can be difficult to dine out with young children. Let's face it. They can be loud and sometimes make a mess. Your only choice seems to be fast food. If you dare go anywhere else, someone is bound to make you feel unwelcome. But here at Wally's Family Restaurant, we welcome families. We offer an extensive kids' menu and lots of coloring books and other activities to keep them busy while you enjoy a healthy meal in a comfortable atmosphere. And best of all, it won't break the bank.

RESPONSE TIME
00:00:45

It can be difficult to dine out with young children. Let's face it. They can be loud and sometimes make a mess. Your only choice seems to be fast food. If you dare go anywhere else, someone is bound to make you feel unwelcome. But here at Wally's Family Restaurant, we welcome families. We offer an extensive kids' menu and lots of coloring books and other activities to keep them busy while you enjoy a healthy meal in a comfortable atmosphere. And best of all, it won't break the bank.

和年幼的孩子在外頭吃飯是件困難的事。面對現實吧。他們可能會非常吵鬧，有時還會弄得一團糟。你唯一的選擇似乎是速食店。如果你敢去別的地方，一定會有人讓你覺得你不受歡迎。但是在威利家庭餐廳這裡，我們歡迎你闔家光臨。我們提供多種兒童餐、大量的著色本和其他活動，讓孩子們一直忙個不停，而你們就可以在舒適的氣氛下，享用健康的一餐。最棒的是，你的荷包不會大失血。

** ─────────────────────

dine out 在外面吃飯 ***Let's face it.*** 面對現實吧。
make a mess 弄得一團糟 dare〔dɛr〕*aux.* 敢
be bound to 一定 unwelcome〔ʌn'wɛlkəm〕*adj.* 不受歡迎的
extensive〔ɪk'stɛnsɪv〕*adj.* 數量多的
coloring book 著色本 atmosphere〔'ætməs,fɪr〕*n.* 氣氛
best of all 最好的是 ***break the bank*** 花大錢

Question 3 : Describe a Picture

Directions: In this part of the test, you will describe the picture on your screen in as much detail as you can. You will have 30 seconds to prepare your response. Then you will have 45 seconds to speak about the picture.

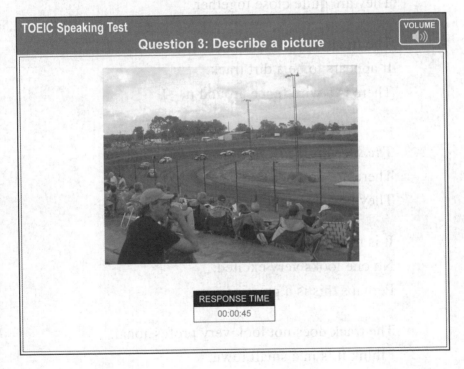

This is a racetrack.
There is a car race going on.
A few people have turned out to watch.

I can see six cars on the track.
They are coming around a curve.
They are quite close together.

The track looks like it is not paved.
It appears to be a dirt track.
There is a wire fence around it.

The spectators are sitting on a hill.
There are no seats.
They have brought their own chairs.

It is not very crowded.
No one looks very excited.
Perhaps this is a practice race.

The track does not look very professional.
I think it is in a small town.
I can see trees on the other side of the track.

中文翻譯

這是一個賽車場。
有一場賽車正在進行。
有一些人來看比賽。

我可以看到有六輛車在賽車道上。
他們正繞過彎道。
他們全都相當接近。

賽車道看起來像是沒有舖過。
它似乎是砂土跑道。
有鐵絲網圍繞著它。

觀眾們正坐在斜坡上。
那裡沒有座位。
他們自己帶椅子來。

那裡不是很擁擠。
沒有人看起來很興奮。
也許這只是一場練習賽。

這個賽車道看起來不是很專業。
我想它是在小鎮裡。
我可以看到賽車道對面還有些樹木。

**

racetrack〔'res,træk〕n. 賽車場　　*go on* 進行　　***turn out*** 出現
track〔træk〕n. 跑道　　***come around a curve*** 轉彎
paved〔pevd〕adj. 舖設好的　　***dirt track*** 砂土跑道
wire〔waɪr〕n. 鐵絲　　fence〔fɛns〕n. 圍籬
spectator〔'spɛktetə〕n. 觀眾　　hill〔hɪl〕n. 斜坡
professional〔prə'fɛʃənl̩〕adj. 專業的

Questions 4-6 : Respond to Questions

⊙ Track 08

Directions: In this part of the test, you will answer three questions. For each question, begin responding immediately after you hear a beep. No preparation time is provided. You will have 15 seconds to respond to Questions 4 and 5 and 30 seconds to respond to Question 6.

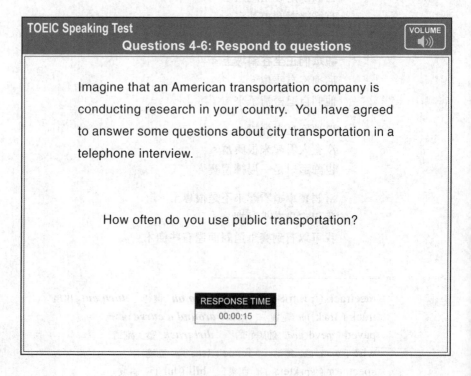

TOEIC Speaking Test
Questions 4-6: Respond to questions
VOLUME 🔊

Imagine that an American transportation company is conducting research in your country. You have agreed to answer some questions about city transportation in a telephone interview.

How often do you use public transportation?

RESPONSE TIME
00:00:15

⇨ Question 5 is on the next page.

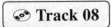 **Track 08**

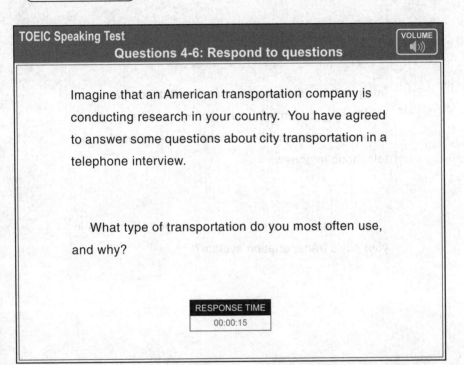

TOEIC Speaking Test

Questions 4-6: Respond to questions

VOLUME

Imagine that an American transportation company is conducting research in your country. You have agreed to answer some questions about city transportation in a telephone interview.

What type of transportation do you most often use, and why?

RESPONSE TIME
00:00:15

⇨ Question 6 is on the next page.

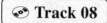

 **Track 08**

TOEIC Speaking Test
VOLUME
Questions 4-6: Respond to questions

Imagine that an American transportation company is
conducting research in your country. You have agreed
to answer some questions about city transportation in a
telephone interview.

What improvements, if any, would you like to see in
your city's transportation system?

RESPONSE TIME
00:00:30

必背答題範例 （ Track 09 ）

Imagine that an American transportation company is conducting research in your country. You have agreed to answer some questions about city transportation in a telephone interview.

想像一下，有一家美國運輸公司正在你的國家進行一項調查。你已同意於電話訪問中，回答一些有關城市交通運輸的問題。

Q4: How often do you use public transportation?
你多久搭一次大眾交通運輸工具？

A4: I use it every day to get to work.
我每天都搭它去上班。
It's a lot more convenient than driving myself.
這比我自己開車方便太多了。
I don't have to worry about parking.
我不必擔心停車的問題。

Q5: What type of transportation do you most often use, and why?
你最常搭乘哪種交通工具，原因為何？

A5: I usually take the bus. 我通常都搭公車。
There is a stop very close to my house.
有一個公車站離我家很近。
It takes me practically door-to-door.
它幾乎直接載我到門口。

** ————————————————

transportation〔͵trænspə'teʃən〕*n.* 運輸工具
conduct〔kən'dʌkt〕*v.* 進行　research〔'risɜtʃ〕*n.* 調查
interview〔'ɪntə͵vju〕*n.* 訪問　parking〔'pɑrkɪŋ〕*n.* 停車
stop〔stɑp〕*n.* 停車站　practically〔'præktɪkḷɪ〕*adv.* 幾乎
door-to-door〔'dɔrtə'dɔr〕*adv.* 門到門地；從一處直接到另一處

Q6: What improvements, if any, would you like to
see in your city's transportation system?

如果有的話,你希望看到你居住的城市的運輸系統有
什麼改善?

A6: I wish the transportation would run later.
The buses stop too early.
The subway stops running before midnight.

If I go out at night, I have to drive.
It's either that or take a taxi.
That can get expensive.

I think a lot of people would agree with me.
We live in a 24/7 city.
We need to be able to get around all the time.

我希望交通運輸工具能營運到晚一點。
公車太早收班了。
地下鐵在午夜前就停止營運了。

如果我晚上要出門,我就必須開車。
不這樣就得搭計程車。
那樣會非常地貴。

我想會有很多人同意我的看法。
我們住在一個不夜城。
我們需要能隨時到達任何地方。

** ─────────────────────

improvement〔ɪm'pruvmənt〕*n.* 改善
run〔rʌn〕*v.* 運轉;進行　　subway〔'sʌb,we〕*n.* 地鐵
24/7(唸成 twenty-four seven)字面的意思是「每天 24 小時,
每週 7 天」,引申為「全天候;不停歇」。
get around 到處走;四處旅行　　***all the time*** 一直;始終

Questions 7-9 : Respond to Questions Using Information Provided

 Track 08

TOEIC Speaking Test

Questions 7-9: Respond to questions using information provided

VOLUME

Directions: In this part of the test, you will answer three questions based on the information provided. You will have 30 seconds to read the information before the questions begin. For each question, begin responding immediately after you hear a beep. No additional preparation time is provided. You will have 15 seconds to respond to Questions 7 and 8 and 30 seconds to respond to Question 9.

TOEIC Speaking Test
Questions 7-9: Respond to questions using information provided

Improve Your Job Skills

Hobart Community College is offering workshops in the following subjects:

> Bookkeeping   Monday, Wednesday
> Word processing   Tuesday, Thursday
> Database management   Tuesday, Friday
> Interview Strategies   Wednesday, Friday

All workshops run for three weeks, from 6 p.m. – 8 p.m.

Fees: $100 per 12-hour course

Registration: March 10 - 15.

Courses begin April 1.

題目解說

【中文翻譯】

增進你的工作技能

荷巴特社區大學即將開設以下科目的進修班：

➤ 簿記　　　　　　　星期一、星期三
➤ 文書處理　　　　　星期二、星期四
➤ 資料庫管理　　　　星期二、星期五
➤ 面試策略　　　　　星期三、星期五

所有進修班都爲期三週，從晚上六點到八點。

費用：每種課程十二小時，共一百美元
報名：三月十日至十五日。
課程從四月一日開始。

【背景敘述】

> Hi, I'm calling about the job skills workshops you have coming up. Can you give me some information?

嗨，我打電話來是想問你們即將開始的工作技能進修班。你能提供我一些資訊嗎？

** ——————————————

improve〔ɪm'pruv〕*v.* 改變；使進步
skill〔skɪl〕*n.* 技能
Hobart〔'ho͵bɑrt〕*n.* 荷巴特
community〔kə'mjunətɪ〕*n.* 社區
workshop〔'wɝk͵ʃɑp〕*n.* 研討會；講習班
subject〔'sʌbdʒɪkt〕*n.* 科目
bookkeeping〔'buk͵kipɪŋ〕*n.* 簿記
word processing 文書處理

database〔'detə͵bes〕*n.* 資料庫
management〔'mænɪdʒmənt〕*n.* 管理
interview〔'ɪntɚ͵vju〕*n.* 面試
strategy〔'strætədʒɪ〕*n.* 策略
run〔rʌn〕*v.* 持續　　fee〔fi〕*n.* 費用
course〔kors〕*n.* 課程
registration〔͵rɛdʒɪ'streʃən〕*n.* 註冊；報名
come up 出現；開始
information〔͵ɪnfɚ'meʃən〕*n.* 資訊

必背答題範例 (**Track 09**)

Q7: How long is each course?

每一種課程時間是多久？

A7: Each course lasts for three weeks.

You meet twice a week for two hours.

That's twelve hours in all.

每一種課程都持續三週。

你每週上課兩次，每次兩小時。

總共是十二個小時。

Q8: How much does it cost and when do I register?

這要花多少錢，還有我要何時報名？

A8: Each workshop costs $100.

Registration starts on March 10.

You need to register by March 15.

每一個進修班的費用是一百美元。

報名從三月十日開始。

你必須在三月十五日前報名。

**─────────────

last〔læst〕*v.* 持續   meet〔mit〕*v.* 上課

in all 總計

register〔ˈrɛdʒɪstə〕*v.* 註冊；報名

by〔baɪ〕*prep.* 在…之前

Q9: I'm looking for a secretarial job. What do you
　　recommend I take?
　　我正在找秘書的工作。你會推薦我修什麼課呢？

A9: I think you should take word processing.
　　It's a good general skill to have.
　　Most managers expect it.

　　There's also the interview strategies class.
　　It's perfect for job seekers.
　　It'll help you land the job you want.

　　The other workshops are good, too.
　　But you can't take them all at once.
　　I'd focus on basic skills first if I were you.

　　我想你應該修文書處理。
　　這是個應該具備的，很好的一般技能。
　　大部分的經理都會希望秘書有這項技能。

　　還有面試策略課程。
　　這對求職者來說最棒了。
　　它可以幫助你得到你想要的工作。

　　其他的進修班也很不錯。
　　但是你無法同時修所有的課。
　　如果我是你，我會先著重在基本技能上。

** ───────────────────

secretarial〔͵sɛkrə'tɛrɪəl〕adj. 秘書的
recommend〔͵rɛkə'mɛnd〕v. 推薦　　take〔tek〕v. 修（課）
general〔'dʒɛnərəl〕adj. 一般的　　manager〔'mænɪdʒɚ〕n. 經理
expect〔ɪk'spɛkt〕v. 預期該有　　*job seeker* 求職者
land〔lænd〕v. 獲得　　*all at once* 同時

Question 10 : Propose a Solution

Track 08

Directions: In this part of the test, you will be presented with a problem and asked to propose a solution. You will have 30 seconds to prepare. Then you will have 60 seconds to speak. In your response, be sure to show that you recognize the problem, and propose a way of dealing with the problem.

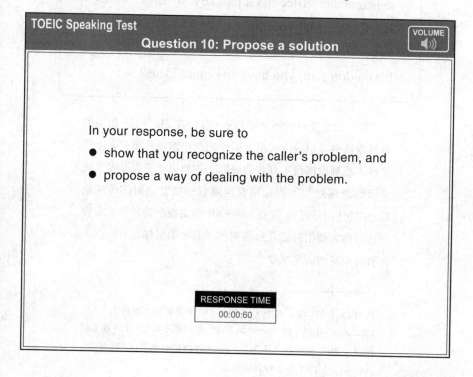

TOEIC Speaking Test

Question 10: Propose a solution

VOLUME

In your response, be sure to
- show that you recognize the caller's problem, and
- propose a way of dealing with the problem.

RESPONSE TIME
00:00:60

➡ Now listen to the voice message.

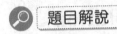

題目解說

【語音留言】

> Hi. This is Agnes Watson. I live in apartment 2B. This is really embarrassing, but I seem to have locked myself out this morning. Anyway, I can't find my keys anywhere. They're probably inside. I was hoping you could help me out. I understand the management office has a passkey for emergencies. If you do, could you call me at 858-9901? I'll meet you at the apartment anytime it's convenient for you. If you don't, do you have any other ideas?

　　嗨。我是艾格妮斯・華特生。我住在 2B 公寓。這眞的是很難爲情，但我今天早上似乎把自己鎖在外面了。不管怎樣，我到處都找不到我的鑰匙。它們可能是在屋內。我希望你能幫助我。我知道管理處有一把緊急用的萬能鑰匙。如果你有的話，能打 858-9901 這支電話給我嗎？我會在任何你方便的時間在公寓與你見面。如果你沒有的話，你有沒有其他的主意呢？

** ───────────

Agnes Watson〔ˋægnɪs ˋwɑtsn̩〕n. 艾格妮斯・華特生
embarrassing〔ɪmˋbærəsɪŋ〕adj. 令人難爲情的；令人尷尬的
lock…out 把…鎖在外面　　***management office*** 管理處
passkey〔ˋpæsˌki〕n. 萬能鑰匙
emergency〔ɪˋmɝdʒənsɪ〕n. 緊急狀況

必背答題範例 (⊙ **Track 09**)

Ms. Watson, this is Jake from Newhill Apartments.
I'm sorry to hear about your trouble.
I'll do what I can to help you get back in.

Please don't feel embarrassed.
It happens more often than you think.
People lock themselves out all the time.

We used to have a passkey, but we don't anymore.
People were concerned about security.
They were afraid of robberies.

You'll probably have to get a locksmith.
There are many listed in the phone book.
I could also give you the name of one.

Another option is to let our maintenance man
    do it.
He can remove the lock from your door.
It wouldn't cost you as much as a locksmith.

But he's not an expert.
You may end up having to buy a new lock.
Let me know what you decide.

中文翻譯

華特生女士，我是新丘公寓的傑克。
得知妳的苦惱，我感到很難過。
我會盡我所能，幫助妳回到屋裡。

請不用感到難為情。
這種事比妳想像中還要常發生。
人們總是把自己給鎖在外面。

我們以前是有萬能鑰匙，但現在沒有了。
人們會擔心安全的問題。
他們擔心會被搶劫。

妳可能必須去找一位鎖匠。
電話簿上列有很多。
我也能給你其中一位的名字。

另一個選擇，就是讓我們的維修人員處理。
他可以移除妳門上的鎖。
花費不會像請鎖匠那麼貴。

但他不是專業人員。
最後妳可能必須買一個新鎖。
讓我知道妳的決定。

**

embarrassed〔ɪm'bærəst〕*adj.* 尷尬的　　***all the time*** 總是
used to 以前　　security〔sɪ'kjʊrətɪ〕*n.* 安全
robbery〔'rɑbərɪ〕*n.* 搶劫　　locksmith〔'lɑk,smɪθ〕*n.* 鎖匠
phone book 電話簿　　maintenance〔'mentənəns〕*n.* 維修
remove〔rɪ'muv〕*v.* 移除　　lock〔lɑk〕*n.* 鎖
expert〔'ɛkspɝt〕*n.* 專家　　***end up V-ing*** 最後…

Question 11 : Express an Opinion

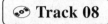 **Track 08**

Directions: In this part of the test, you will give your opinion about a specific topic. Be sure to say as much as you can in the time allowed. You will have 15 seconds to prepare. Then you will have 60 seconds to speak.

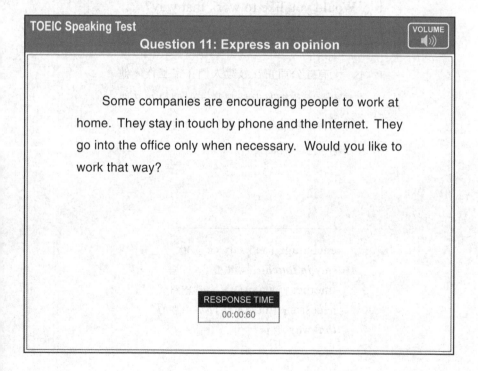

TOEIC Speaking Test

Question 11: Express an opinion

VOLUME

Some companies are encouraging people to work at home. They stay in touch by phone and the Internet. They go into the office only when necessary. Would you like to work that way?

RESPONSE TIME
00:00:60

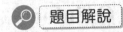

題目解說

> Some companies are encouraging people to work at home. They stay in touch by phone and the Internet. They go into the office only when necessary. Would you like to work that way?

　　有些公司正在鼓勵人們在家工作。他們用電話和網路保持聯繫。他們只在必要時才會進辦公室。你會想要用這種方式工作嗎？

**　**** ────────────────

encourage〔 ɪnˋkɝɪdʒ 〕 v. 鼓勵
stay in touch 保持聯繫
Internet〔ˋɪntɚ͵nɛt 〕 n. 網際網路
necessary〔ˋnɛsə͵sɛrɪ 〕 adj. 必要的
that way 那樣

I would have to think seriously about that.
There are both advantages and disadvantages.
It wouldn't be an easy decision.

Working from home could save a lot of time.
I wouldn't have to commute into the city.
I could sleep late or do other things.

It would also be very comfortable.
I wouldn't have to wear a suit.
I could take a break whenever I wanted.

On the other hand, the work might take longer to do.
It could be tough to concentrate.
There are lots of distractions at home.

In addition, I'd rarely see my colleagues.
I might feel lonely working all alone.
It might be tough to stay motivated.

All things considered, I don't think I'd like it.
I'd rather work in an office.
I'd rather keep my home life separate.

中文翻譯

我得認真地思考這個問題。
這有利也有弊。
這不是個容易的決定。

在家工作可以省下很多時間。
我不需要通勤到城市裡。
我可以睡晚一點或者做些別的事。

在家工作也會很舒服。
我不需要穿套裝。
什麼時候想休息都可以。

但另一方面，工作可能要更久才能完成。
在家工作會很難專心。
家裡有太多令人分心的東西。

除此之外，我會很少見到我的同事。
獨自工作，我可能會感到孤單。
這樣很難保持動力。

考量一切情形後，我想我不喜歡這樣。
我寧可在辦公室裡工作。
我寧願讓家裡生活和工作分開。

** _____

seriously〔'sɪrɪəslɪ〕*adv.* 認真地　　advantage〔əd'væntɪdʒ〕*n.* 優點
disadvantage〔,dɪsəd'væntɪdʒ〕*n.* 缺點
commute〔kə'mjut〕*v.* 通勤　　suit〔sut〕*n.* 西裝；套裝
tough〔tʌf〕*adj.* 困難的　　concentrate〔'kɑnsn̩,tret〕*v.* 專心
distraction〔dɪ'strækʃən〕*n.* 使人分心的事物
all alone 獨自一人　　motivated〔'motə,vetɪd〕*adj.* 有動力的
all things considered 考量一切情形後

TOEIC Speaking Test ⑤

Question 1: Read a Text Aloud

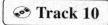 **Track 10**

Directions: In this part of the test, you will read aloud the text on the screen. You will have 45 seconds to prepare. Then you will have 45 seconds to read the text aloud.

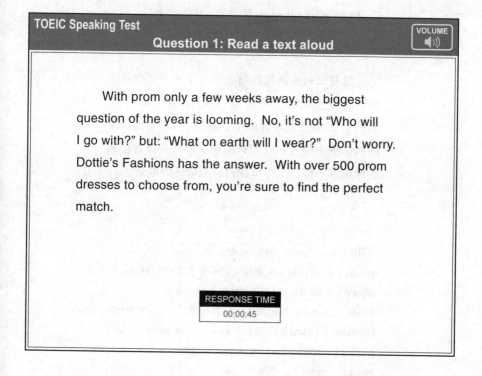

TOEIC Speaking Test

Question 1: Read a text aloud

VOLUME

With prom only a few weeks away, the biggest question of the year is looming. No, it's not "Who will I go with?" but: "What on earth will I wear?" Don't worry. Dottie's Fashions has the answer. With over 500 prom dresses to choose from, you're sure to find the perfect match.

RESPONSE TIME
00:00:45

題目解說 (**Track 11**)

> With prom only a few weeks away, the biggest question of the year is looming. No, it's not "Who will I go with?" but: "What on earth will I wear?" Don't worry. Dottie's Fashions has the answer. With over 500 prom dresses to choose from, you're sure to find the perfect match.

　　舞會只剩幾個禮拜就要舉行了，今年最重大的問題隱隱浮現。不，不是「我要跟誰一起去？」而是：「我到底要穿什麼？」別擔心。多蒂流行服飾為你提供解答。我們有超過五百件的舞會服裝供你選擇，你一定可以找到最適合你的服裝。

** ────────────

with〔 wɪθ 〕 *prep.* 因為；由於
prom〔 prɑm 〕 *n.* (大學生、高中生舉辦的) 舞會
away〔 ə'we 〕 *adv.* 【用於名詞後】離…多久
loom〔 lum 〕 *v.* 隱約出現；陰森地逼近　　***on earth*** 究竟
fashion〔'fæʃən 〕 *n.* 流行；時裝　　***be sure to*** 必定
perfect〔'pɜfɪkt 〕 *adj.* 完美的；完全的
match〔 mætʃ 〕 *n.* 相配的人或物

Question 2 : Read a Text Aloud

Track 10

Directions: In this part of the test, you will read aloud the text on the screen. You will have 45 seconds to prepare. Then you will have 45 seconds to read the text aloud.

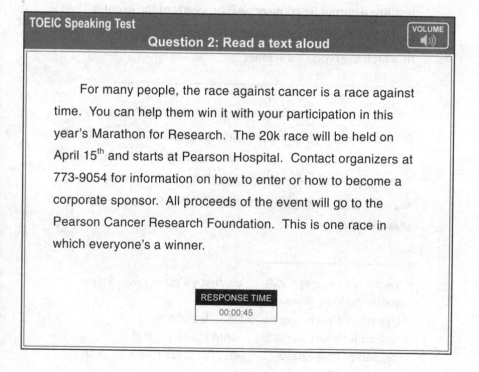

TOEIC Speaking Test

Question 2: Read a text aloud

VOLUME

For many people, the race against cancer is a race against time. You can help them win it with your participation in this year's Marathon for Research. The 20k race will be held on April 15th and starts at Pearson Hospital. Contact organizers at 773-9054 for information on how to enter or how to become a corporate sponsor. All proceeds of the event will go to the Pearson Cancer Research Foundation. This is one race in which everyone's a winner.

RESPONSE TIME
00:00:45

題目解說　(✆ **Track 11**)

For many people, the race against cancer is a race against time. You can help them win it with your participation in this year's Marathon for Research. The 20k race will be held on April 15th and starts at Pearson Hospital. Contact organizers at 773-9054 for information on how to enter or how to become a corporate sponsor. All proceeds of the event will go to the Pearson Cancer Research Foundation. This is one race in which everyone's a winner.

對許多人而言，對抗癌症的競賽，就是與時間的競賽。你可以參與今年的研究馬拉松，來幫助他們贏得比賽。這個二十公里的賽跑將於四月十五日舉行，並於皮爾森醫院起跑。打 773-9054 與主辦單位聯絡，取得如何參加或如何成為共同贊助人的資訊。這項活動的所有收益，都將捐給皮爾森癌症研究基金會。這是一場人人皆是贏家的比賽。

**

---

race〔 res 〕*n.* 比賽；賽跑　　against〔 ə'gɛnst 〕*prep.* 對抗
participation〔 pɚ͵tɪsə'peʃən 〕*n.* 參與
marathon〔'mærə͵θɑn 〕*n.* 馬拉松；長距離賽跑
research〔'risɝtʃ 〕*n.* 研究　　hold〔 hold 〕*v.* 舉辦
organizer〔'ɔrgə͵naɪzɚ 〕*n.* 主辦人　　enter〔'ɛntɚ 〕*v.* 參加
corporate〔'kɔrpərɪt 〕*adj.* 共同的
sponsor〔'spɑnsɚ 〕*n.* 贊助者　　proceeds〔'prosidz 〕*n. pl.* 收益
event〔 ɪ'vɛnt 〕*n.* 大型活動　　***go to*** 歸於
foundation〔 faun'deʃən 〕*n.* 基金會　　winner〔'wɪnɚ 〕*n.* 贏家

Question 3 : Describe a Picture

Track 10

Directions: In this part of the test, you will describe the picture on your screen in as much detail as you can. You will have 30 seconds to prepare your response. Then you will have 45 seconds to speak about the picture.

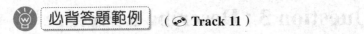
必背答題範例 (**Track 11**)

This is a picture of a gas station.
Its name is Conoco.
It's located on a suburban street.

There is also a convenience store.
It's located behind the gas pumps.
Its name is Tri-Mart.

There is a big sign in front of the pumps.
It lists the price of gas.
The station sells three types of fuel.

The station isn't very busy.
There are only three vehicles at the pumps.
One is a car; another is a minivan.

I don't see any people.
I think maybe it is a self-service station.
There are no attendants to pump gas.

The drivers of the cars might be inside.
They might be paying the bill.
They might be buying some snacks.

中文翻譯

這是一座加油站的照片。
它的名字是科諾克。
它位於郊區的街上。

還有一間便利商店。
它位於加油機的後面。
它的名字是三合一市場。

加油機前面有個大招牌。
它列出汽油的價錢。
這座加油站賣三種燃料。

這座加油站不是很熱鬧。
只有三輛車在加油機旁邊。
一輛是小客車；另一輛是小貨車。

我沒有看到任何人。
我想這也許是座自助式加油站。
沒有服務人員在加油。

汽車的駕駛人可能在裡面。
他們可能在付錢。
他們可能在買一些點心。

**

gas〔gæs〕*n.* 汽油（ = *gasoline* ）   ***gas station*** 加油站
located〔'loketɪd〕*adj.* 位於…的   suburban〔sə'bɝbən〕*adj.* 郊外的
pump〔pʌmp〕*n.* 幫浦 *v.* 注入…   ***gas pump*** 加油機
mart〔mɑrt〕*n.* 市場   fuel〔'fjuəl〕*n.* 燃料   busy〔'bɪzɪ〕*adj.* 熱鬧的
vehicle〔'viɪkl̩〕*n.* 車輛   minivan〔'mɪnɪˌvæn〕*n.* 小貨車
self-service〔'sɛlf'sɝvɪs〕*adj.* 自助的   attendant〔ə'tɛndənt〕*n.* 服務員
pump gas 加油   ***pay the bill*** 付帳   snack〔snæk〕*n.* 點心

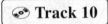

Questions 4-6 : Respond to Questions

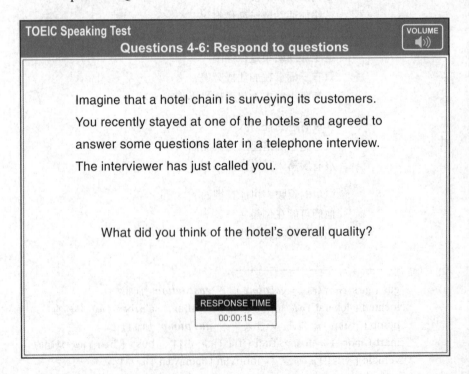

Track 10

Directions: In this part of the test, you will answer three questions. For each question, begin responding immediately after you hear a beep. No preparation time is provided. You will have 15 seconds to respond to Questions 4 and 5 and 30 seconds to respond to Question 6.

TOEIC Speaking Test

Questions 4-6: Respond to questions

VOLUME

Imagine that a hotel chain is surveying its customers. You recently stayed at one of the hotels and agreed to answer some questions later in a telephone interview. The interviewer has just called you.

What did you think of the hotel's overall quality?

RESPONSE TIME
00:00:15

⇨ Question 5 is on the next page.

Track 10

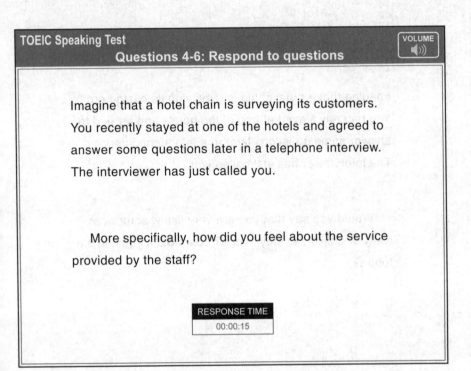

TOEIC Speaking Test

Questions 4-6: Respond to questions

VOLUME

Imagine that a hotel chain is surveying its customers.
You recently stayed at one of the hotels and agreed to
answer some questions later in a telephone interview.
The interviewer has just called you.

More specifically, how did you feel about the service
provided by the staff?

RESPONSE TIME
00:00:15

⇨ Question 6 is on the next page.

 Track 10

TOEIC Speaking Test

Questions 4-6: Respond to questions

VOLUME

Imagine that a hotel chain is surveying its customers. You recently stayed at one of the hotels and agreed to answer some questions later in a telephone interview. The interviewer has just called you.

Would you say that you are very likely, somewhat likely or unlikely to stay in one of our hotels again in the future?

RESPONSE TIME

00:00:30

必背答題範例 (**Track 11**)

Imagine that a hotel chain is surveying its customers. You recently stayed at one of the hotels and agreed to answer some questions later in a telephone interview. The interviewer has just called you.

想像一下，有家連鎖旅館正在對它的顧客做調查。你最近住過其中一家旅館，並同意之後在電話訪問中回答一些問題。電訪員剛打電話給你。

Q4: What did you think of the hotel's overall quality?
你認為旅館整體的品質如何？

A4: I thought it was fine. 我覺得很好。
The room was clean. 房間很乾淨。
It was also pretty quiet. 也非常安靜。

Q5: More specifically, how did you feel about the service provided by the staff?
更精確地說，你對工作人員提供的服務覺得如何？

A5: They were very helpful and polite.
他們肯主動幫忙並且很有禮貌。
The desk clerk gave us some information about local restaurants.
櫃台人員給了我們一些當地餐廳的資訊。
We really appreciated that. 我們真的很感激。

** ————————————————

chain〔tʃen〕 *n.* 連鎖店　　survey〔sɚ've〕 *v.* 調查
recently〔'risn̩tlɪ〕 *adv.* 最近　　stay〔ste〕 *v.* 暫住
interviewer〔'ɪntɚˌvjuɚ〕 *n.* 探訪者　　overall〔'ovɚˌɔl〕 *adj.* 整體的
specifically〔spɪ'sɪfɪkl̩ɪ〕 *adv.* 明確地　　staff〔stæf〕 *n.* 工作人員
helpful〔'hɛlpfəl〕 *adj.* 主動幫忙的　　desk〔dɛsk〕 *n.* (旅館的) 櫃台
clerk〔klɝk〕 *n.* 職員　　appreciate〔ə'priʃɪˌet〕 *v.* 感激

Q6: Would you say that you are very likely,
somewhat likely or unlikely to stay in one of
our hotels again in the future?
在未來，你認為你非常可能、有可能，或是不可能再
次光臨我們其中一家旅館？

A6: I'm likely to choose your hotel again.
To be honest, it depends on the price.
I usually look for the best deal.

But your hotels are in good locations.
Most are close to the highway or the city center.
That counts for a lot.

Other things being equal, I'd stay there again.
It was good value for the money.
I was very satisfied.

我有可能再次選擇你們的旅館。
老實說，這視價錢而定。
我通常會尋找最便宜的價格。

不過你們的旅館地點很好。
大部分都離公路或市中心很近。
這非常重要。

如果其他條件都一樣，我會再度住那裡。
以這個價錢來說是很划算的。
我非常滿意。

**

say〔se〕v. 認為　likely〔'laɪklɪ〕adj. 可能的
somewhat〔'sʌmˌhwɑt〕adv. 有點
unlikely〔ʌn'laɪklɪ〕adj. 不可能的　*the best deal* 最划算的交易
count for a lot 很有價值　equal〔'ikwəl〕adj. 相等的；同樣的
be good value for the money 以這個價格來說是很划算的

Questions 7-9 : Respond to Questions Using Information Provided

Track 10

TOEIC Speaking Test
 Questions 7-9: Respond to questions using information provided

VOLUME

Directions: In this part of the test, you will answer three questions based on the information provided. You will have 30 seconds to read the information before the questions begin. For each question, begin responding immediately after you hear a beep. No additional preparation time is provided. You will have 15 seconds to respond to Questions 7 and 8 and 30 seconds to respond to Question 9.

Employee Orientation

When: Monday, August 29
Where: Meeting Room 1
Who: All employees hired within the last 4 weeks

9:00   **Welcome**
        Polly Hart, Human Resources
9:30   **Company Overview**
        Ted Wasserstern, Public Relations
10:00   **Benefits** (insurance, vacation, retirement, etc.)
        Nan Simmons, Human Resources
10:30   **Introduction of Department Heads**

        coffee break

11:00   **Tour of the Facilities**
12:00   **Lunch**

Please note that attendance by all new employees is required.
Should you be unable to attend for any reason, please contact
Stan Altman in Human Resources, ext 405

【中文翻譯】

新進員工訓練

時間：八月二十九日，星期一
地點：第一會議室
對象：過去四週內雇用之所有員工

9:00　歡迎會
　　　波莉·哈特，人力資源部
9:30　公司概況
　　　泰德·瓦瑟斯坦，公關部
10:00　福利（保險、休假、退休等）
　　　南·賽門斯，人力資源部
10:30　部長介紹

休息時間

11:00　參觀設備
12:00　午餐

請注意，所有新進員工都必須出席。若有任何原因無法出席，請與人力資源部的史丹·奧特曼聯絡，分機號碼為405

【背景敘述】

> Hi! This is Joe McAllister. I've just joined the customer service department. I understand you're pretty new here, too. Can I ask you a few questions?

嗨！我是喬‧麥卡利斯特。我剛加入客服部。我知道你在這邊也算蠻新的。我可以問你一些問題嗎？

** ————————————————

employee〔͵ɛmplɔɪˋi〕 *n.* 員工
orientation〔͵orɪɛnˋteʃən〕 *n.* (新進人員的) 訓練；指導
hire〔haɪr〕 *v.* 雇用   resource〔rɪˋsors〕 *n.* 資源
human resources 人力資源部
overview〔ˋovɚ͵vju〕 *n.* 概要   ***public relations*** 公共關係
benefits〔ˋbɛnəfɪts〕 *n. pl.* 福利
insurance〔ɪnˋʃʊrəns〕 *n.* 保險

retirement〔rɪˋtaɪrmənt〕 *n.* 退休   ***etc.*** 等等 (= *et cetera*)
introduction〔͵ɪntrəˋdʌkʃən〕 *n.* 介紹
head〔hɛd〕 *n.* 首長   ***coffee break*** 休息時間
tour〔tʊr〕 *n.* 遊覽；參觀   facilities〔fəˋsɪlətɪz〕 *n. pl.* 設備
note〔not〕 *v.* 注意   attendance〔əˋtɛndəns〕 *n.* 出席；參加
required〔rɪˋkwaɪrd〕 *adj.* 必須的
attend〔əˋtɛnd〕 *v.* 出席；參加   ***ext*** 分機 (= *extension*)
customer service 客戶服務

必背答題範例 (🕉 **Track 11**)

Q7: Is there any type of orientation or training for
new employees?

有沒有任何形式的新進員工指導或訓練？

A7: Yes, there is.

It's on Monday, August 29.

It starts at 9:00 in Meeting Room 1.

有。

在八月二十九號，星期一。

從九點開始，在第一會議室。

Q8: What if we can't make it that day?

如果我們當天不能來怎麼辦？

A8: Actually, it's required.

I'm sure your manager will let you go.

If not, you should call Human Resources and
tell them.

事實上，必須要來。

我確定你的經理會讓你去。

如果不去的話，你應該打電話給人力資源部，告訴他們。

**　**

＊＊ ────────────────

training (ˈtrenɪŋ) *n.* 訓練　　***What if~?*** ～該怎麼辦？

make it 辦到；能去　　actually (ˈæktʃʊəlɪ) *adv.* 事實上

manager (ˈmænɪdʒɚ) *n.* 經理

Q9: What's going to happen at the orientation?

在訓練新進人員時會有什麼事？

A9: First they'll welcome us.

Polly Hart will give a speech.

I think she's the head of Human Resources.

Then we'll learn about the company.

After that, Nan Simmons will talk about benefits.

Then we meet the department heads.

After a break, we take a tour.

Finally, we have lunch.

I suppose we go back to work in the afternoon.

首先他們會歡迎我們。

波莉‧哈特會演講。

我想她是人力資源部的部長。

然後我們會得知公司的相關資訊。

在那之後，南‧賽門斯會說有關福利的事。

然後我們會見到各部門的部長。

休息過後，我們會參觀一下。

最後，我們會吃中餐。

我猜我們下午會回去工作。

**

give a speech 演講　 learn〔lɜn〕v. 知道

take a tour 去參觀

suppose〔sə'poz〕v. 推測；猜想

Question 10 : Propose a Solution

Track 10

Directions: In this part of the test, you will be presented with a problem and asked to propose a solution. You will have 30 seconds to prepare. Then you will have 60 seconds to speak. In your response, be sure to show that you recognize the problem, and propose a way of dealing with the problem.

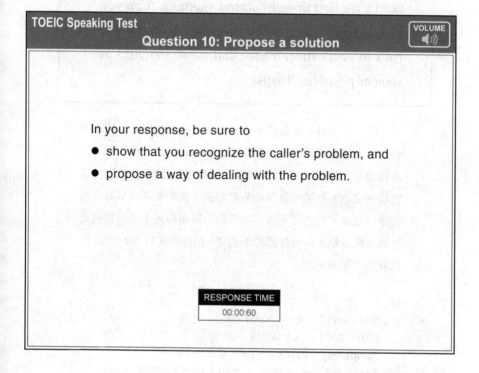

TOEIC Speaking Test

Question 10: Propose a solution

VOLUME

In your response, be sure to
- show that you recognize the caller's problem, and
- propose a way of dealing with the problem.

RESPONSE TIME
00:00:60

➡ Now listen to the voice message.

【語音留言】

> Hi. This is Dan Myers. I rented a car from you this morning. I'm calling to tell you that we've had some problems with it. It wasn't running well and stalled often. We got it back to the hotel, but now it's completely dead. It won't even start. We really need a car first thing tomorrow morning. Can you give us a new one? But I can't even drive this one back to your office. Please call me at 566-9023 as soon as possible. Thanks.

嗨。我是丹・麥爾斯。我今天早上向你們租了一輛車。我打來是要告訴你們，我們在用這輛車時出了一些問題。它運轉得不是很好，而且常常熄火。我們把它開回旅館，但是它現在完全不動了。連發動都沒辦法。我們明天一早真的很需要一輛車。你們可不可以給我們一輛新的呢？但是我甚至沒辦法將這輛車開回你們的辦公室。請你們快打 566-9023 和我聯絡。謝謝。

**

rent〔rɛnt〕*v.* 租　　run〔rʌn〕*v.* 運轉
stall〔stɔl〕*v.* 熄火；拋錨
completely〔kəm'plitlɪ〕*adv.* 完全地
dead〔dɛd〕*adj.* 不動的　　start〔stɑrt〕*v.* 發動
first thing 一早

必背答題範例 (● Track 11)

Hello, *Mr. Myers*.

This is Dawn from Altamont Motors.

I'm returning your call.

I'm sorry to hear about your car.

This is very unusual.

We rarely get complaints about the cars.

But we'll take care of it right away.

We'll replace the car for you.

We'll even give you an upgrade.

Don't worry about getting the car to our office.

We'll send someone to pick it up.

We'll come to your hotel.

Your new car will be in the parking lot by 6 p.m.

We'll leave the keys with the manager.

You don't have to wait around for us.

I'm very sorry you were inconvenienced.

I hope you enjoy your new car.

Please let me know if you need any other
   assistance.

中文翻譯

哈囉，麥爾斯先生。
我是亞特蒙汽車公司的道恩。
我是要回覆您的電話。

聽到您的行車狀況，我很抱歉。
這是非常少見的。
我們很少接到對車子的抱怨。

但是我們會立刻處理這件事。
我們會換一輛車給您。
我們甚至會給您升級。

不用擔心把車開回我們辦公室的事。
我們會派人去拿車。
我們會去您的旅館。

您的新車會在晚上六點前停放在停車場內。
我們會將鑰匙留給經理。
您就不用空等我們了。

給您帶來不便，我很抱歉。
希望您喜歡您的新車。
如果您還需要任何其他的協助，請讓我知道。

** ───────────────

motor〔ˋmotɚ〕 *n.* 汽車　　unusual〔ʌnˋjuʒʊəl〕 *adj.* 罕見的
rarely〔ˋrɛrlɪ〕 *adv.* 很少　　complaint〔kəmˋplent〕 *n.* 抱怨
take care of 處理　　replace〔rɪˋples〕 *v.* 更換
upgrade〔ˋʌpˋgred〕 *n.* 升級　　***pick up*** （把東西）取走
parking lot 停車場　　***wait around*** 空等
inconvenience〔ˏɪnkənˋvinjəns〕 *v.* 使感到不便
assistance〔əˋsɪstəns〕 *n.* 幫助

Question 11 : Express an Opinion

Track 10

Directions: In this part of the test, you will give your opinion about a specific topic. Be sure to say as much as you can in the time allowed. You will have 15 seconds to prepare. Then you will have 60 seconds to speak.

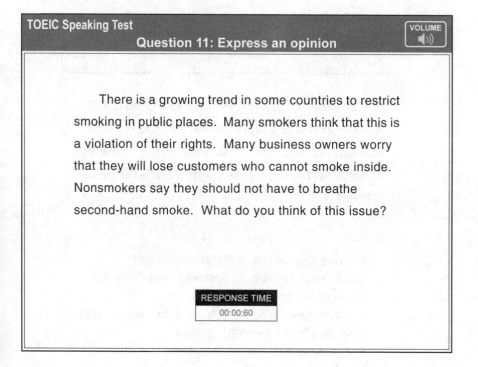

TOEIC Speaking Test
Question 11: Express an opinion
VOLUME

There is a growing trend in some countries to restrict smoking in public places. Many smokers think that this is a violation of their rights. Many business owners worry that they will lose customers who cannot smoke inside. Nonsmokers say they should not have to breathe second-hand smoke. What do you think of this issue?

RESPONSE TIME
00:00:60

題目解說

> There is a growing trend in some countries to restrict smoking in public places. Many smokers think that this is a violation of their rights. Many business owners worry that they will lose customers who cannot smoke inside. Nonsmokers say they should not have to breathe second-hand smoke. What do you think of this issue?

在某些國家,限制公共場所不得吸煙的趨勢愈來愈明顯。許多吸煙者認為這侵害了他們的權利。許多商家擔心他們會流失無法在室內吸煙的顧客。不吸煙的人則說他們本來就不該吸二手煙。你對這個問題有何看法?

** ————————————

growing〔'groɪŋ〕adj. 在增加的;愈來愈強的
trend〔trɛnd〕n. 趨勢　　restrict〔rɪ'strɪkt〕v. 限制
smoker〔'smokɚ〕n. 吸煙者
violation〔ˌvaɪə'leʃən〕n. 侵害　　right〔raɪt〕n. 權利
business〔'bɪznɪs〕n. 商店;公司行號
nonsmoker〔nɑn'smokɚ〕n. 不抽煙的人
breathe〔brið〕v. 呼吸
second-hand〔'sɛkənd'hænd〕adj. 二手的
smoke〔smok〕n. 煙　　issue〔'ɪʃu〕n. 問題;議題

必背答題範例   (**Track 11**)

I am a smoker.

I think it is my right to smoke.

However, I agree that there should be limitations.

Second-hand smoke really bothers some people.

Some are even allergic.

It can have a serious effect on their health.

So I think it should not be allowed in some places.

Most restaurants and offices do not have enough
    fresh air.

Nonsmokers cannot escape the smoke.

Yet I think some nonsmokers go too far.

They want to stop smoking everywhere.

They even want to stop it outdoors.

I think we need to share our space.

We need to compromise on this issue.

We should all respect the rights of others.

The limitations should be reasonable.

Smoking should be banned only in enclosed
    spaces.

It should be allowed where it cannot bother
    anyone.

中文翻譯

我是個吸煙者。
我認為吸煙是我的權利。
然而，我同意應該要有個限制。

二手煙的確會干擾到某些人。
有些人甚至會過敏。
這可能會對他們的健康造成嚴重的影響。

所以我認為在某些地方不該允許抽煙。
大部分的餐廳和辦公室都沒有足夠的新鮮空氣。
不吸煙的人無法逃離煙味。

但是我認為有些不吸煙的人太過份了。
他們想要在每個地方都禁煙。
他們甚至想在戶外禁煙。

我認為我們必須共享我們的空間。
我們必須在這個問題上妥協。
我們都該尊重別人的權利。

限制必須合情合理。
應該只在密閉空間禁止吸煙。
在不會干擾任何人的地方，應該要被允許。

**

limitation〔,lɪmə'teʃən〕n. 限制　　bother〔'baðɚ〕v. 打擾
allergic〔ə'lɝdʒɪk〕adj. 過敏的　　fresh〔frɛʃ〕adj. 新鮮的
escape〔ə'skep〕v. 逃避　　**go too far** 太過份了
stop〔stɑp〕v. 阻止　　space〔spes〕n. 空間；場所；地區
compromise〔'kɑmprə,maɪz〕v. 妥協
respect〔rɪ'spɛkt〕v. 尊重　　reasonable〔'riznəbḷ〕adj. 合理的
ban〔bæn〕v. 禁止　　enclosed〔ɪn'klozd〕adj. 密閉的

TOEIC Speaking Test ⑥

Question 1: Read a Text Aloud

 **Track 12**

Directions: In this part of the test, you will read aloud the text on the screen. You will have 45 seconds to prepare. Then you will have 45 seconds to read the text aloud.

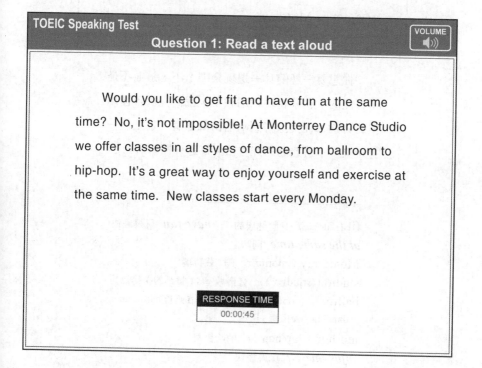

TOEIC Speaking Test

Question 1: Read a text aloud

VOLUME

Would you like to get fit and have fun at the same time? No, it's not impossible! At Monterrey Dance Studio we offer classes in all styles of dance, from ballroom to hip-hop. It's a great way to enjoy yourself and exercise at the same time. New classes start every Monday.

RESPONSE TIME
00:00:45

題目解說 (♪ Track 13)

Would you like to get fit and have fun at the same time? No, it's not impossible! At Monterrey Dance Studio we offer classes in all styles of dance, from ballroom to hip-hop. It's a great way to enjoy yourself and exercise at the same time. New classes start every Monday.

你想要一邊健身一邊玩樂嗎？不，這並不是不可能的！在蒙特瑞舞蹈教室，我們提供各種類型的舞蹈，從交際舞到嘻哈街舞都有。這是個一邊玩樂、一邊運動的好方法。每週一開新班。

**

fit〔fɪt〕adj. 身體健康的　　*have fun* 玩得愉快
at the same time 同時
Monterrey〔ˌmɑntə're〕n. 蒙特瑞
studio〔'stjudɪˌo〕n. 音樂教室；(舞蹈的) 排練房
ballroom〔'bɔlˌrum〕n. 舞廳【在此指 ballroom
　　dancing「交際舞」】
hip-hop〔'hɪp'hɑp〕n. 嘻哈街舞
enjoy oneself 玩得愉快
exercise〔'ɛksəˌsaɪz〕v. 運動

Question 2 : Read a Text Aloud

 **Track 12**

Directions: In this part of the test, you will read aloud the text on the screen. You will have 45 seconds to prepare. Then you will have 45 seconds to read the text aloud.

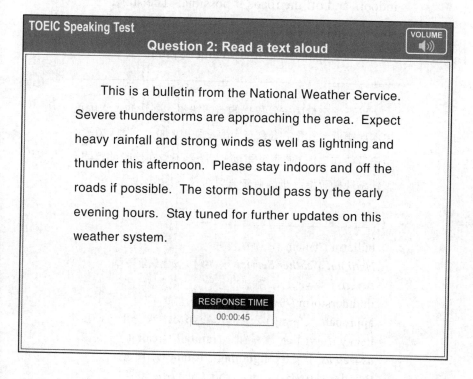

TOEIC Speaking Test

Question 2: Read a text aloud

VOLUME

This is a bulletin from the National Weather Service. Severe thunderstorms are approaching the area. Expect heavy rainfall and strong winds as well as lightning and thunder this afternoon. Please stay indoors and off the roads if possible. The storm should pass by the early evening hours. Stay tuned for further updates on this weather system.

RESPONSE TIME
00:00:45

題目解說 （ **Track 13** ）

> This is a bulletin from the National Weather
> Service. Severe thunderstorms are approaching the
> area. Expect heavy rainfall and strong winds as well
> as lightning and thunder this afternoon. Please stay
> indoors and off the roads if possible. The storm
> should pass by the early evening hours. Stay tuned
> for further updates on this weather system.

　　以下是來自國家氣象局的新聞快報。強烈的大雷雨正
往本地接近。預計午後會有大雨及強風，加上打雷、閃電。
請儘量待在室內，並避免開車上路。暴風會在傍晚前離開。
請繼續收聽更進一步的最新氣象報導。

** ————————————————

bulletin（ˈbʊlətn̩ ）*n.* 新聞快報
National Weather Service （美國）國家氣象局
severe（ səˈvɪr ）*adj.* 強烈的
thunderstorm（ˈθʌndɚˌstɔrm ）*n.* 大雷雨
approach（ əˈprotʃ ）*v.* 接近　　expect（ ɪkˈspɛkt ）*v.* 預計
heavy（ˈhɛvɪ ）*adj.* 猛烈的　　rainfall（ˈrenˌfɔl ）*n.* 降雨
as well as 以及　　lightning（ˈlaɪtnɪŋ ）*n.* 閃電
thunder（ˈθʌndɚ ）*n.* 雷　　off（ ɔf ）*prep.* 離開
if possible 如果可能的話　　storm（ stɔrm ）*n.* 暴風雨
stay tuned 繼續收聽　　further（ˈfɝðɚ ）*adj.* 更進一步的
update（ˈʌpdet ）*n.* 最新情報　　***weather system*** 天氣系統

Question 3 : Describe a Picture

Directions: In this part of the test, you will describe the picture on your screen in as much detail as you can. You will have 30 seconds to prepare your response. Then you will have 45 seconds to speak about the picture.

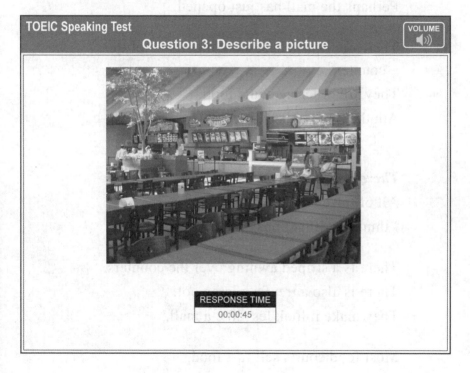

必背答題範例 (**Track 13**)

This is a food court.

I think it's in a shopping mall.

I can see three different sellers.

The place is practically empty.

It must be very early.

Perhaps the mall has just opened.

There are two people standing at one of the counters.

They are ordering some food.

Another person is eating.

There are several very long tables.

All of the chairs are empty except one.

I think it will get busy later.

There is a striped awning over the counters.

There is also a tree in a large pot.

They make it look less like a mall.

Most food courts sell fast food.

There is always a wide variety.

It's very popular with shoppers.

中文翻譯

這是一個美食廣場。
我認為它位於購物中心裡面。
我可以看到三個不同的攤位。

這個地方幾乎是空蕩蕩的。
時間一定還很早。
也許購物中心才剛開始營業。

有兩個人站在其中一個櫃台前。
他們正在點餐。
另一個人正在用餐。

有幾張很長的桌子。
所有的椅子都沒人坐，除了一張以外。
我想晚一點將會變熱鬧。

在櫃台的上方有條紋樣式的遮篷。
還有一棵在大花盆裡的樹。
它們讓這裡看起來比較不像購物中心。

美食廣場大多都賣速食。
總是有很多的種類。
非常受顧客的歡迎。

** ─────────────────────

food court （購物中心裡的）美食廣場
shopping mall 購物中心　　seller〔ˋsɛlɚ〕 n. 賣方
practically〔ˋpræktɪklɪ〕 adv. 幾乎　　counter〔ˋkauntɚ〕 n. 櫃台
busy〔ˋbɪzɪ〕 adj. 熱鬧的　　striped〔straɪpt〕 adj. 有條紋的
awning〔ˋɔnɪŋ〕 n. 遮篷　　pot〔pɑt〕 n. 花盆　*fast food* 速食
variety〔vəˋraɪətɪ〕 n. 種類；多樣性　*a wide variety* 種類很多
be popular with 受～歡迎　　shopper〔ˋʃɑpɚ〕 n. 顧客

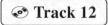

Questions 4-6 : Respond to Questions

>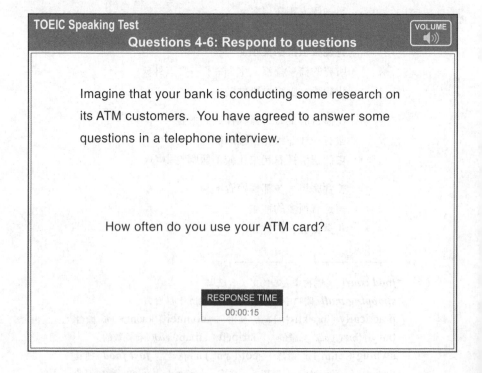

Directions: In this part of the test, you will answer three questions. For each question, begin responding immediately after you hear a beep. No preparation time is provided. You will have 15 seconds to respond to Questions 4 and 5 and 30 seconds to respond to Question 6.

TOEIC Speaking Test
VOLUME 🔊

Questions 4-6: Respond to questions

Imagine that your bank is conducting some research on its ATM customers. You have agreed to answer some questions in a telephone interview.

How often do you use your ATM card?

RESPONSE TIME
00:00:15

⇨ Question 5 is on the next page.

Track 12

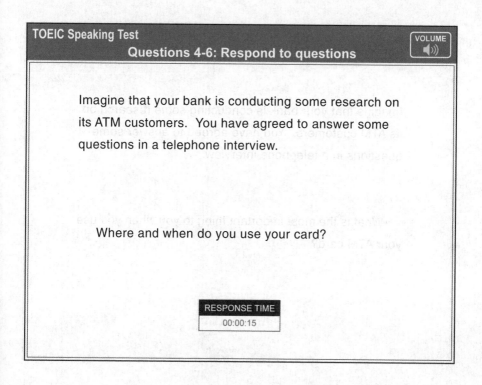

⇨ Question 6 is on the next page.

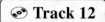
Track 12

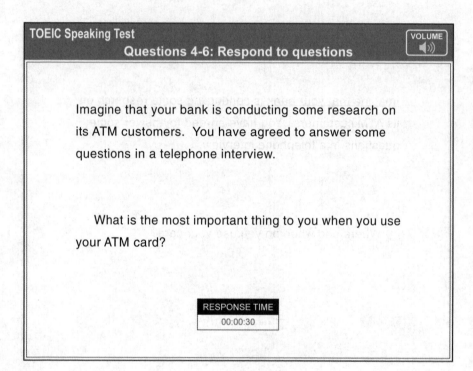

TOEIC Speaking Test

Questions 4-6: Respond to questions

VOLUME

Imagine that your bank is conducting some research on
its ATM customers. You have agreed to answer some
questions in a telephone interview.

What is the most important thing to you when you use
your ATM card?

RESPONSE TIME
00:00:30

必背答題範例 （ Track 13 ）

　　Imagine that your bank is conducting some research on its ATM customers.　You have agreed to answer some questions in a telephone interview.

　　想像一下，你的銀行正在對使用自動提款機的顧客進行調查。你已同意於電話訪問中回答一些問題。

Q4： How often do you use your ATM card?
　　　你多久使用一次提款卡？

A4： I use it once or twice a week, sometimes more.
　　　我每週使用一到二次，有時候更多。
　　　It depends on what I'm doing. 要看我在做什麼。
　　　It's nice to have when I have unexpected expenses.
　　　當我有超出預期的支出時，有提款卡很方便。

Q5： Where and when do you use your card?
　　　你會在何處及何時使用你的提款卡？

A5： I often use it when I go shopping.
　　　我常在我去購物時使用。
　　　So I use the ATMs in malls.
　　　所以我會使用購物中心裡的自動提款機。
　　　I also use it when the bank is closed.
　　　我也在銀行結束營業時使用。

** ────────────

imagine〔ɪˋmædʒɪn〕 *v.* 想像
conduct〔kənˋdʌkt〕 *v.* 進行　　research〔ˋrisɝtʃ〕 *n.* 調查
ATM 自動提款機（ = *automated teller machine* ）
interview〔ˋɪntɚˏvju〕 *n.* 訪問　　***depend on*** 視…而定
unexpected〔ˏʌnɪkˋspɛktɪd〕 *adj.* 意外的
expense〔ɪkˋspɛns〕 *n.* 費用

Q6: What is the most important thing to you when you use your ATM card?

當你在使用提款卡時，對你而言什麼最重要？

A6: The most important thing to me is security.
I'm always afraid that someone else will get into my account.
I'm afraid my money will disappear.

I might lose my card someday.
Or it might get stolen.
I want to be able to cancel it right away.

I also want the ATMs to be secure.
I'm afraid of hidden cameras.
I try hard to protect my PIN number.

對我而言，安全最重要。
我總是擔心帳戶會被別人入侵。
我怕我的錢會不翼而飛。

我可能會在某一天遺失我的卡片。
或者它可能會被偷。
我希望能立即將它取消。

我也希望自動提款機能夠很安全。
我很怕隱藏式攝影機。
我非常努力地保護我的密碼。

** ─────────────────────

security〔sɪ'kjʊrətɪ〕*n.* 安全   account〔ə'kaʊnt〕*n.* 帳戶
disappear〔ˌdɪsə'pɪr〕*v.* 消失   lose〔luz〕*v.* 遺失
someday〔'sʌm,de〕*adv.*（將來）有一天
secure〔sɪ'kjʊr〕*adj.* 安全的   ***hidden camera*** 隱藏式攝影機
PIN number 個人識別碼；密碼（= *personal identification number*）

Questions 7-9 : Respond to Questions Using Information Provided

Track 12

TOEIC Speaking Test
Questions 7-9: Respond to questions using information provided

VOLUME

Directions: In this part of the test, you will answer three questions based on the information provided. You will have 30 seconds to read the information before the questions begin. For each question, begin responding immediately after you hear a beep. No additional preparation time is provided. You will have 15 seconds to respond to Questions 7 and 8 and 30 seconds to respond to Question 9.

Fullton Library Pancake Breakfast

The Fullton Library is holding its annual pancake breakfast on Sunday, June 10. All proceeds will go to the Books for Kids fund. Books for Kids is a non-profit organization that supplies new and used books to kids in underprivileged neighborhoods. The Fullton library has been a longtime supporter of the program thanks to the donations and efforts of its members.

Breakfast will be served buffet style on the library grounds. In case of rain, the event will be postponed until the following Sunday, June 17.

Time: 9:00 a.m.-11:00 a.m., June 10

Cost: $5 for adults; $2.50 for children under 12

【中文翻譯】

福爾頓圖書館煎餅早餐會

　　福爾頓圖書館將在六月十日星期日，舉辦一年一度的煎餅早餐會。所有收益將捐給「給孩子的書」作為基金。「給孩子的書」是一個非營利組織，提供新舊書籍給貧困地區的小孩。福爾頓圖書館是這個計劃長期的支持者，這都要感謝會員們的捐贈與努力。

　　早餐將於圖書館廣場上，以自助方式供應。若遇雨天，活動將延至下禮拜天，即六月十七日。

　　時間：六月十日，早上九點至十一點
　　費用：成人五美元；十二歲以下兒童二元五角

【背景敘述】

> Hi, I heard that the library is going to be holding a breakfast next month. Can I ask you a few questions about it?

嗨，我聽說圖書館下個月將要舉辦早餐會。
我可以問你一些相關問題嗎？

** ────────────

pancake ('pæn,kek) *n.* 薄煎餅　　hold (hold) *v.* 舉行
annual ('ænjuəl) *adj.* 一年一度的
proceeds ('prosidz) *n. pl.* 收益
go to 歸於　　fund (fʌnd) *n.* 基金
non-profit (,nɑn'prɑfɪt) *adj.* 非營利性的
organization (,ɔrgənə'zeʃən) *n.* 組織
supply (sə'plaɪ) *v.* 提供
used (juzd) *adj.* 用過的；舊的；二手的
underprivileged (,ʌndə'prɪvəlɪdʒd) *adj.* 貧困的

neighborhood ('nebə,hud) *n.* 地區
longtime ('lɔŋ'taɪm) *adj.* 長期的
supporter (sə'portə) *n.* 支持者　　***thanks to*** 由於；幸虧
donation (do'neʃən) *n.* 捐贈　　effort ('ɛfət) *n.* 努力
serve (sɝv) *v.* 供應　　buffet (bu'fe) *adj.* 自助餐式的
grounds (graundz) *n. pl.* 廣場
in case of 如果發生　　event (ɪ'vɛnt) *n.* 大型活動
postpone (post'pon) *v.* 延期
following ('falɔɪŋ) *adj.* 其次的；接著的

必背答題範例 （ **Track 13** ）

Q7: Where and when will it be held?

將在何時何地舉行？

A7: It's on June 10th.

It starts at nine and runs till eleven.

It's going to be outdoors at the library.

在六月十日。

九點開始，一直進行到十一點。

將在圖書館的室外舉行。

Q8: How much does it cost?

費用是多少？

A8: It's five dollars for adults, two-fifty for kids.

For that price you get all the pancakes you

　　can eat.

And all the money goes to charity.

大人五美元，小孩二塊五美元。

以這樣的價格，煎餅隨你吃到飽。

所有的錢都會捐給慈善機構。

**
run〔rʌn〕*v.* 進行

charity〔'tʃærətɪ〕*n.* 慈善團體

Q9: Who does the money go to?

這些錢會捐給誰？

A9: The event is for a charity.

It's called Books for Kids.

It brings books to poor children.

It's a non-profit organization.

So it depends on donations.

The library has supported it for years.

It's a very worthy cause.

It's helped a lot of children.

We'd really appreciate your support.

這項活動是為了一個慈善機構舉辦的。

它叫作「給孩子的書」。

它將書籍帶給貧困兒童。

它是個非營利組織。

所以它仰賴別人的捐款。

這家圖書館已經支持它好多年了。

這是一個非常有意義的活動。

它幫助了很多孩童。

我們會非常感激你的支持。

** ————————————————

depend on 依賴　　worthy〔ˋwɝðɪ〕*adj.* 有價值的

cause〔kɔz〕*n.* 運動；主張；目的

appreciate〔əˋpriʃɪˌet〕*v.* 感激

Question 10 : Propose a Solution

Track 12

Directions: In this part of the test, you will be presented with a problem and asked to propose a solution. You will have 30 seconds to prepare. Then you will have 60 seconds to speak. In your response, be sure to show that you recognize the problem, and propose a way of dealing with the problem.

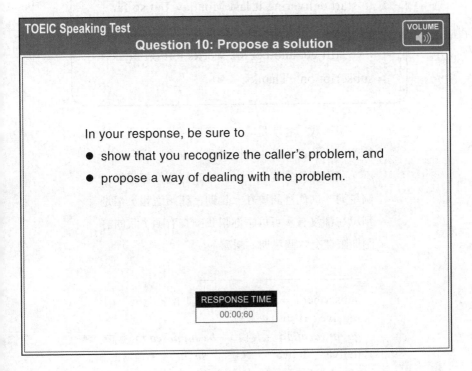

> TOEIC Speaking Test
>
> **Question 10: Propose a solution**
>
> VOLUME
>
> In your response, be sure to
> - show that you recognize the caller's problem, and
> - propose a way of dealing with the problem.
>
> RESPONSE TIME
> 00:00:60

➡ Now listen to the voice message.

題目解說

【語音留言】

> Hi. My name is Harry Jones. I'm a subscriber to your newspaper. I'm calling because I haven't been receiving my paper. I went on vacation last month, and I stopped the paper for two weeks. You were supposed to start delivering it last Monday, but so far no paper. Could you check into this for me? I've still got another six weeks left on my subscription. Thanks.

　　嗨。我的名字是哈利・瓊斯。我有訂閱你們的報紙。我打電話來是因為我一直沒收到我的報紙。我上個月去度假,所以停止訂閱你們報紙兩個星期。你們應該要在上星期一開始送報,但是到現在都沒有。可以請你幫我查查看嗎?我的訂閱期限還有六個星期。謝謝。

** ————————————————

subscriber〔səb'skraɪbɚ〕n. 訂閱者 < to >
receive〔rɪ'siv〕v. 收到
go on vacation 去度假　　*be supposed to* 應該
deliver〔dɪ'lɪvɚ〕v. 遞送　　*so far* 到目前為止
check into 調查　　left〔lɛft〕adj. 剩下的
subscription〔səb'skrɪpʃən〕n. 訂閱

 **(Track 13)**

Hello, Mr. Jones.
This is Maggie at The Morning News.
I'm returning your call.

I'm very sorry about the mix-up with your paper.
You should have received it this week.
The mistake is due to a clerical error.

The clerk entered your return date incorrectly.
We thought you were coming back next week.
That's why we haven't delivered your paper.

We're going to start delivering your paper tomorrow.
It should be there at the usual time.
If it's not, please give me a call.

In addition, we're going to extend your
   subscription.
We're going to give you another two weeks free.
That's to apologize for our mistake.

I see you are a longtime subscriber to our paper.
We really value your loyalty.
I hope you continue to enjoy the paper.

中文翻譯

哈囉，瓊斯先生。

我是早晨日報的梅姬。

我是要回覆您的電話。

對於您的報紙所出的錯，我很抱歉。

您應該在這個星期就收到報紙。

這個錯誤是因為職員的疏失。

職員將您回來的日期輸入錯誤。

我們以為您下星期才會回來。

這就是我們還沒送報紙給您的原因。

我們將在明天開始送報給您。

應該會在照往常的時間到達。

如果沒有，請打電話給我。

此外，我們將會延長您的訂閱期限。

我們將免費送您兩個禮拜的報紙。

這是要為我們的錯誤道歉。

我知道您長久以來一直訂閱我們的報紙。

我們非常重視您的忠誠。

希望您能繼續喜愛我們的報紙。

** ────────────────

return〔rɪˋtɝn〕*v.* 回覆　*adj.* 回來的　　mix-up〔ˋmɪksˏʌp〕*n.* 混亂

clerical〔ˋklɛrɪkḷ〕*adj.* 職員的　　error〔ˋɛrɚ〕*n.* 錯誤

clerk〔klɝk〕*n.* 職員　　incorrectly〔ˏɪnkəˋrɛktlɪ〕*adv.* 錯誤地

give sb. a call 打電話給某人　　***in addition*** 此外

extend〔ɪkˋstɛnd〕*v.* 延長　　free〔fri〕*adv.* 免費地

apologize〔əˋpɑləˏdʒaɪz〕*v.* 道歉　　value〔ˋvæljʊ〕*v.* 重視

loyalty〔ˋlɔɪəltɪ〕*n.* 忠實；忠誠　　enjoy〔ɪnˋdʒɔɪ〕*v.* 喜愛

Question 11 : Express an Opinion

Track 12

Directions: In this part of the test, you will give your opinion about a specific topic. Be sure to say as much as you can in the time allowed. You will have 15 seconds to prepare. Then you will have 60 seconds to speak.

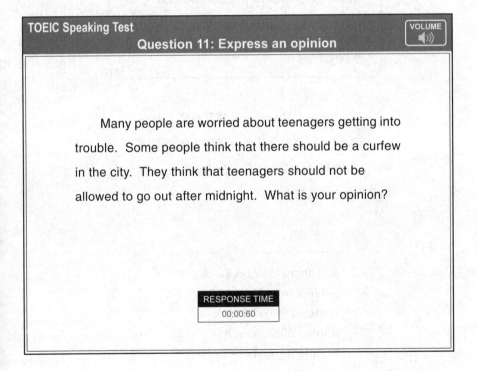

TOEIC Speaking Test
Question 11: Express an opinion

VOLUME

Many people are worried about teenagers getting into trouble. Some people think that there should be a curfew in the city. They think that teenagers should not be allowed to go out after midnight. What is your opinion?

RESPONSE TIME
00:00:60

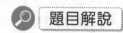 題目解說

Many people are worried about teenagers getting into trouble. Some people think that there should be a curfew in the city. They think that teenagers should not be allowed to go out after midnight. What is your opinion?

許多人擔心青少年愛惹麻煩。有些人認為都市裡應該要有宵禁。他們認為不應該允許青少年在午夜過後外出。你的意見為何？

**

teenager (ˈtinˌedʒɚ) *n.* 青少年
get into trouble 惹麻煩
curfew (ˈkɝfju) *n.* 宵禁
allow (əˈlaʊ) *v.* 允許
midnight (ˈmɪdˌnaɪt) *n.* 午夜
opinion (əˈpɪnjən) *n.* 意見

必背答題範例   (⊘ Track 13)

I think a curfew is not necessary.
Most teenagers are not as bad as people think.
Only a few of them cause trouble.

Teens looking for trouble would just ignore the
   curfew anyway.
They would find a way to go out.
It wouldn't change their behavior.

I think the parents should be responsible.
They should know where their children are.
They should be in control.

A curfew would keep the police busy.
It would waste their time.
They have more important things to worry about.

If they caught a teenager, they'd have to take
   him in.
It wouldn't matter if he was doing anything
   wrong or not.
It would be the law.

The teens could get a police record.
That could affect their future.
A curfew could cause a lot of problems for
   everyone.

中文翻譯

我認爲宵禁是沒有必要的。
大部份的青少年並不如大家所想的那麼惡劣。
只有其中的一些會惹是生非。

會惹麻煩的青少年，無論如何都不會把宵禁當一回事。
他們會想辦法出門。
這不會改變他們的行爲。

我認爲父母應該負起責任。
他們應該要知道他們的孩子在哪裡。
他們應該要掌控一切。

宵禁會讓警察很忙碌。
這會浪費他們的時間。
他們有更重要的事要煩惱。

如果他們抓到青少年，他們就必須拘留他。
這與他是否做錯事無關。
這就是法律。

青少年會有前科紀錄。
那會影響他們的未來。
宵禁可能會爲大家帶來很多問題。

＊＊ ————————————

necessary〔ˋnɛsə͵sɛrɪ〕*adj.* 必要的　　***look for trouble*** 找麻煩

ignore〔ɪgˋnor〕*v.* 忽視　　anyway〔ˋɛnɪ͵we〕*adv.* 無論如何

behavior〔bɪˋhevjɚ〕*n.* 行爲

responsible〔rɪˋspɑnsəbḷ〕*adj.* 應負責的

in control 掌管著；控制著

keep〔kip〕*v.* 使（人）保持（在某種狀態）　　***worry about*** 擔憂

take in 拘留　　***police record*** 前科紀錄　　affect〔əˋfɛkt〕*v.* 影響

TOEIC Speaking Test ⑦

Question 1: Read a Text Aloud

 **Track 14**

Directions: In this part of the test, you will read aloud the text on the screen. You will have 45 seconds to prepare. Then you will have 45 seconds to read the text aloud.

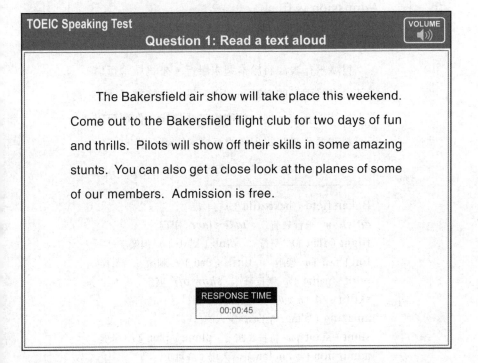

TOEIC Speaking Test
VOLUME

Question 1: Read a text aloud

The Bakersfield air show will take place this weekend. Come out to the Bakersfield flight club for two days of fun and thrills. Pilots will show off their skills in some amazing stunts. You can also get a close look at the planes of some of our members. Admission is free.

RESPONSE TIME
00:00:45

題目解說 (Track 15)

> The Bakersfield air show will take place this weekend. Come out to the Bakersfield flight club for two days of fun and thrills. Pilots will show off their skills in some amazing stunts. You can also get a close look at the planes of some of our members. Admission is free.

　　貝城飛行表演將於本週末舉行。來貝城飛行俱樂部,享受兩天的樂趣和刺激。飛行員將透過一些驚人的特技表演,展現他們的專業技術。你還可以近距離觀看我們某些會員的飛機。入場免費。

** —————————

Bakersfield〔'bekɚzfild〕 *n.* 貝城
air show 飛行表演　　***take place*** 舉行
flight〔flaɪt〕 *n.* 飛行　　club〔klʌb〕 *n.* 俱樂部
fun〔fʌn〕 *n.* 樂趣　　thrill〔θrɪl〕 *n.* 刺激
pilot〔'paɪlət〕 *n.* 飛行員　　***show off*** 展示
skill〔skɪl〕 *n.* (專門) 技能;技術
amazing〔ə'mezɪŋ〕 *adj.* 驚人的
stunt〔stʌnt〕 *n.* 特技表演　　plane〔plen〕 *n.* 飛機
admission〔əd'mɪʃən〕 *n.* 入場 (許可)
free〔fri〕 *adj.* 免費的

Question 2 : Read a Text Aloud

Track 14

Directions: In this part of the test, you will read aloud the text on the screen. You will have 45 seconds to prepare. Then you will have 45 seconds to read the text aloud.

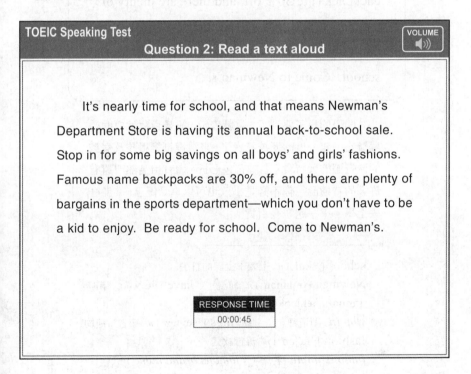

TOEIC Speaking Test
VOLUME

Question 2: Read a text aloud

It's nearly time for school, and that means Newman's Department Store is having its annual back-to-school sale. Stop in for some big savings on all boys' and girls' fashions. Famous name backpacks are 30% off, and there are plenty of bargains in the sports department—which you don't have to be a kid to enjoy. Be ready for school. Come to Newman's.

RESPONSE TIME
00:00:45

題目解說 (🔊 Track 15)

> It's nearly time for school, and that means Newman's Department Store is having its annual back-to-school sale. Stop in for some big savings on all boys' and girls' fashions. Famous name backpacks are 30% off, and there are plenty of bargains in the sports department—which you don't have to be a kid to enjoy. Be ready for school. Come to Newman's.

開學的日子要到了，這就表示，紐曼百貨就要開始舉辦它一年一度的返校特賣了。來這裡逛逛男孩及女孩的流行服飾大特賣。名牌背包七折，體育用品部門還有許多的特價品—你不必是小孩也可以享受優惠。準備好去上學。來一趟紐曼百貨。

** ───────────────

school〔skul〕*n.* 上課；上課的日子
Newman〔'njumən〕*n.* 紐曼　　have〔hæv〕*v.* 舉辦
annual〔'ænjʊəl〕*adj.* 一年一度的
stop in 順道拜訪　　savings〔'sevɪŋz〕*n.* 節省；節約
fashion〔'fæʃən〕*n.* 流行款式
famous name 名牌 (= *famous brand name*)
backpack〔'bæk͵pæk〕*n.* 背包　　***plenty of*** 很多
bargain〔'bɑrgɪn〕*n.* 便宜貨；特價品
sports〔sports〕*adj.* 運動的
department〔dɪ'pɑrtmənt〕*n.* 部門

Question 3 : Describe a Picture

Track 14

Directions: In this part of the test, you will describe the picture on your screen in as much detail as you can. You will have 30 seconds to prepare your response. Then you will have 45 seconds to speak about the picture.

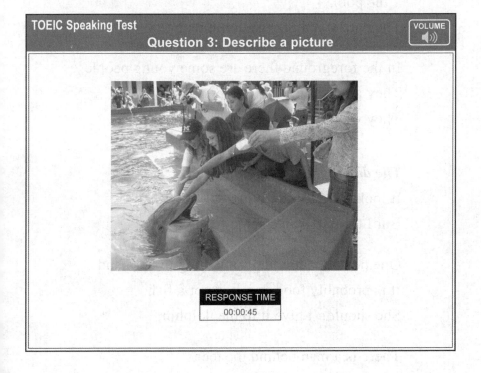

必背答題範例　(**Track 15**)

Some people are petting a dolphin.
I think they are at a marine park.
It's probably in a Western country.

The dolphin is in a pool.
There are a lot of people standing around
　the pool.
They are watching the dolphins.

In the foreground there are some young people.
They are leaning over the pool.
They want to touch the dolphin's head.

The dolphin has its mouth open.
It looks like it is smiling.
But I think it wants some food.

One person is holding something in her hand.
It is probably food, but it is not a fish.
She shouldn't give it to the dolphin.

There is a man behind the teens.
He is holding a camera.
He is taking a picture.

中文翻譯

有些人在摸海豚。
我想他們是在海洋公園。
這可能是在西方國家。

海豚在水池裡。
有很多人圍著水池站著。
他們正在看海豚。

照片前面有一些年輕人。
他們把身體傾向水池。
他們想要摸海豚的頭。

海豚把嘴張得開開的。
看起來好像在笑一樣。
但我想牠是想要一些食物。

有個人手上拿著某樣東西。
那可能是食物，不過不是魚。
她不應該拿食物給海豚。

有位男士站在這些青少年的後面。
他拿著一台照相機。
他正在拍照。

**　———————————————————————————

pet〔pɛt〕v. 撫摸　　dolphin〔'dɑlfɪn〕n. 海豚
marine〔mə'rin〕adj. 海洋的　　pool〔pul〕n. 水池
foreground〔'for,graʊnd〕n. 前景；最前面
lean〔lin〕v.（向前）傾身　　have〔hæv〕v. 使…保持（在某種狀態）
teens〔tinz〕n. pl.（十三到十九歲的）青少年（= teenagers）
camera〔'kæmərə〕n. 照相機　　*take a picture*　照相

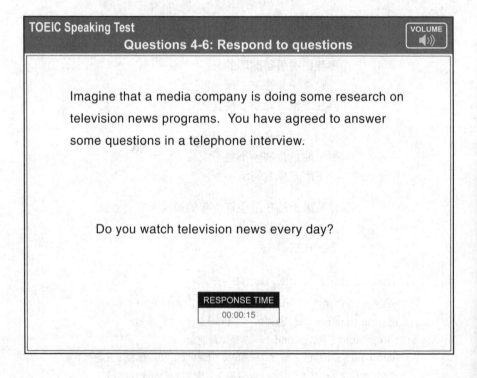

Questions 4-6 : Respond to Questions

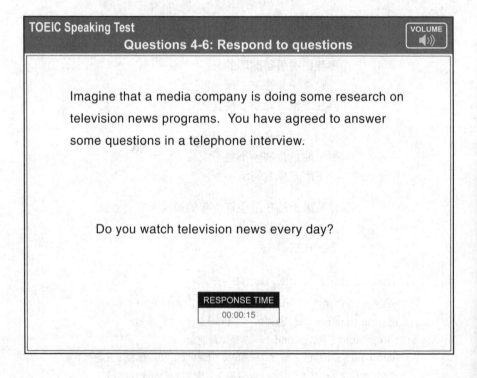 **Track 14**

Directions: In this part of the test, you will answer three questions. For each question, begin responding immediately after you hear a beep. No preparation time is provided. You will have 15 seconds to respond to Questions 4 and 5 and 30 seconds to respond to Question 6.

TOEIC Speaking Test

VOLUME 🔊

Questions 4-6: Respond to questions

Imagine that a media company is doing some research on television news programs. You have agreed to answer some questions in a telephone interview.

Do you watch television news every day?

RESPONSE TIME
00:00:15

⇨ Question 5 is on the next page.

Track 14

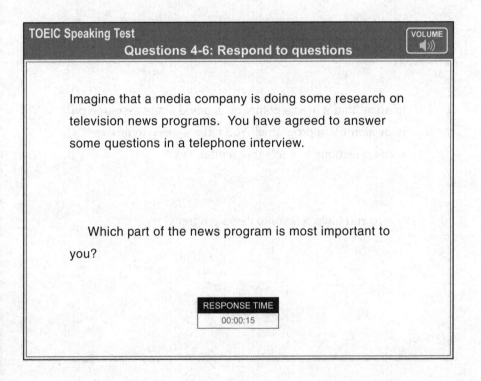

TOEIC Speaking Test

Questions 4-6: Respond to questions

VOLUME

Imagine that a media company is doing some research on television news programs. You have agreed to answer some questions in a telephone interview.

Which part of the news program is most important to you?

RESPONSE TIME
00:00:15

⇨ Question 6 is on the next page.

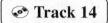 **Track 14**

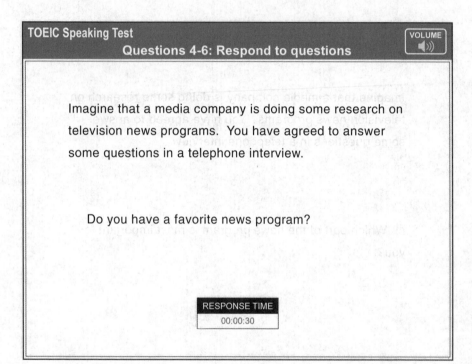

TOEIC Speaking Test

Questions 4-6: Respond to questions

VOLUME

Imagine that a media company is doing some research on television news programs. You have agreed to answer some questions in a telephone interview.

Do you have a favorite news program?

RESPONSE TIME
00:00:30

必背答題範例 (Track 15)

Imagine that a media company is doing some research on television news programs. You have agreed to answer some questions in a telephone interview.

想像一下，有家媒體公司正在進行有關電視新聞節目的調查。你已同意於電話訪問中回答一些問題。

Q4: Do you watch television news every day?
你每天都看電視新聞嗎？

A4: I usually do. 我通常都會看。
I like to watch it in the evening before dinner.
我喜歡在傍晚吃晚餐前收看。
I like to keep up with what's going on.
我喜歡即時掌握時事。

Q5: Which part of the news program is most important to you?
哪一部份的新聞節目對你來說最重要？

A5: I'd have to say the local news.
我必須說是地方新聞。
I want to know what's happening in my city.
我想知道我的城市裡發生了什麼事。
That is what will affect me most.
那才是會對我影響最大的事。

** ————————————————

imagine〔ɪˈmædʒɪn〕v. 想像   media〔ˈmidɪə〕n. pl. 媒體
research〔ˈrisɝtʃ〕n. 調查   interview〔ˈɪntɚˌvju〕n. 訪談
keep up with 跟上；對～消息靈通   ***go on*** 發生
local〔ˈlokḷ〕adj. 地方的   affect〔əˈfɛkt〕v. 影響

Q6: Do you have a favorite news program?

你有特別喜愛的新聞節目嗎？

A6: I like the 6:00 news on Channel 8.

I watch it nearly every day.

I prefer it to the news on other channels.

The newsreaders on Channel 8 are very professional.

I don't want to hear a lot of boring jokes and chat.

I want to know the news.

I like their in-depth stories.

I trust what they say.

That's why I watch them.

我喜歡第八頻道六點的新聞。

我幾乎每天都看。

我喜歡它勝於其他頻道的新聞。

第八頻道的新聞播報員非常專業。

我不想要聽到一大堆無聊的笑話和閒聊。

我想知道新聞。

我喜歡他們深入的報導。

我相信他們所說的。

這是我看他們的原因。

**

channel〔'tʃænḷ〕 *n.* 頻道　　nearly〔'nɪrlɪ〕 *adv.* 幾乎

prefer〔prɪ'fɝ〕 *v.* 比較喜歡　***prefer…to~*** 喜歡…勝於~

newsreader〔'njuz,ridɚ〕 *n.* 新聞報導員

professional〔prə'fɛʃənḷ〕 *adj.* 專業的

chat〔tʃæt〕 *n.* 閒聊　　in-depth〔'ɪn'dɛpθ〕 *adj.* 深入的

story〔'storɪ〕 *n.*（新聞）報導　　trust〔trʌst〕 *v.* 信任

Questions 7-9 : Respond to Questions Using Information Provided

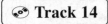 **Track 14**

TOEIC Speaking Test | VOLUME
Questions 7-9: Respond to questions using information provided

Directions: In this part of the test, you will answer three questions based on the information provided. You will have 30 seconds to read the information before the questions begin. For each question, begin responding immediately after you hear a beep. No additional preparation time is provided. You will have 15 seconds to respond to Questions 7 and 8 and 30 seconds to respond to Question 9.

Recycling Schedule

All residents are required to separate their garbage and place recyclables outside on the appropriate day for pickup.

Newspapers	*Monday*
Plastic and Styrofoam	*Wednesday*
Metal cans	*2ⁿᵈ and 4ᵗʰ Thursday*
Glass containers	*1ˢᵗ and 3ʳᵈ Friday*

Please note that the recycling companies will make their pickups between 3 p.m. and 5 p.m. You may place your collection outside in the morning, but please do not put it out the night before. Leaving garbage outside at night attracts animals.

Thank you for your cooperation and remember to reuse and recycle whenever possible!

題目解說

【中文翻譯】

資源回收時間表

所有居民都必須做垃圾分類,並將可回收垃圾於適當的日期置於門外,以利收集。

報紙	*星期一*
塑膠製品和保麗龍	*星期三*
金屬罐	*每月第二及第四個星期四*
玻璃容器	*每月第一及第三個星期五*

請注意,回收公司會在下午三點到五點之間,進行回收工作。你可以將收集好的回收物品,在早上拿到外面,但請不要在前一天晚上就拿出來。晚上將垃圾置於門外,會引來動物。

感謝你的合作,請記得儘可能回收再利用!

【背景敘述】

Hi! This is Alex Andersen. I live down the street from you. We just moved in last week. Anyway, I was wondering if you could give me some information about the recycling program.

　　嗨！我是亞力克斯・安德森。我和你們住在同一條街上。我們上週才剛搬來。不管怎樣，不知道你是否能給我一些關於回收預定表的資訊。

**

recycling〔ˏriˈsaɪklɪŋ〕*n.* 回收
schedule〔ˈskɛdʒul〕*n.* 時間表；計劃表
resident〔ˈrɛzədənt〕*n.* 居民
required〔rɪˈkwaɪrd〕*adj.* 必須的
separate〔ˈsɛpəˏret〕*v.* 把…分類
garbage〔ˈgɑrbɪdʒ〕*n.* 垃圾　　place〔ples〕*v.* 放置
recyclable〔riˈsaɪkləbḷ〕*n.* 可回收利用的東西
appropriate〔əˈproprɪɪt〕*adj.* 適當的
pickup〔ˈpɪkˏʌp〕*n.* 收集

plastic〔ˈplæstɪk〕*n.* 塑膠製品
Styrofoam〔ˈstaɪrəˏfom〕*n.* 保麗龍
metal〔ˈmɛtḷ〕*adj.* 金屬製的　　can〔kən〕*n.* 罐子
container〔kənˈtenɚ〕*n.* 容器　　note〔not〕*v.* 注意
collection〔kəˈlɛkʃən〕*n.* 收集物
cooperation〔koˏɑpəˈreʃən〕*n.* 合作
reuse〔riˈjuz〕*v.* 再利用　　recycle〔riˈsaɪkḷ〕*v.* 回收
down〔daʊn〕*prep.* 沿著　　***move in*** 住進新居
program〔ˈprogræm〕*n.* 計劃；預定表

必背答題範例 （ Track 15 ）

Q7: What kinds of things can I recycle?

哪些種類的東西可以回收？

A7: There are four different categories.

They are newspapers, plastic, metal and glass.

Each one gets picked up on a different day.

有四種不同的種類。

分別是報紙、塑膠製品、金屬和玻璃。

每種的回收日都不同。

Q8: Does someone pick them up every week?

每週都會有人來回收嗎？

A8: Newspapers and plastic are picked up once
   a week.

The others are picked up every other week.

There are no pickups on weekends, though.

報紙和塑膠類每週收一次。

其他則是隔週收一次。

但是週末沒有回收。

** ————————————————

category〔'kætə,gorɪ〕*n.* 種類　　metal〔'mɛtḷ〕*n.* 金屬

get〔gɛt〕*v.* 被…　***pick up*** 把～帶走

every other week 每隔一週；每兩週

though〔ðo〕*adv.*【置於句尾】不過

Q9: So when can I put out my metal cans?
所以我可以在什麼時候把金屬罐放在外面？

A9: You can put them out this Thursday.
It's the fourth Thursday of the month.
Metal is picked up on the second and fourth
  Thursdays.

The truck will come between three and five.
You can put them out earlier if you have to work.
A lot of people do that.

Don't put them out the night before, though.
It's not allowed.
It would attract animals.

你可以在這個星期四把它們放在外面。
那天是本月的第四個星期四。
金屬類會在每月的第二及第四個星期四回收。

卡車會在三點到五點之間過來。
如果你要上班，你可以早一點把它們放在外面。
很多人都這樣做。

但是不要在前一天晚上就把它們放在外面。
這是不被允許的。
這會引來動物。

**────────────

allow 〔ə'laʊ〕 v. 允許

Question 10 : Propose a Solution

Track 14

Directions: In this part of the test, you will be presented with a problem and asked to propose a solution. You will have 30 seconds to prepare. Then you will have 60 seconds to speak. In your response, be sure to show that you recognize the problem, and propose a way of dealing with the problem.

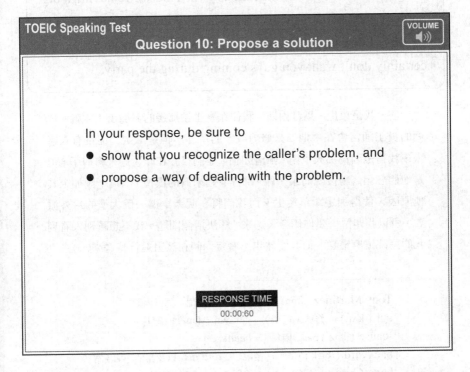

TOEIC Speaking Test
Question 10: Propose a solution

VOLUME

In your response, be sure to
● show that you recognize the caller's problem, and
● propose a way of dealing with the problem.

RESPONSE TIME
00:00:60

➡ Now listen to the voice message.

題目解說

【語音留言】

Hi. This is Tony Martinez. I live at 124 Maple Street over in Huntington. Your people usually come and cut my lawn on Tuesdays, but no one came last Tuesday…I guess 'cause it was raining. Anyway, they finally came yesterday and cut, but they forgot to do part of the backyard. It really looks terrible 'cause the grass is so long after the rain and all. And we're having a big outdoor party tomorrow, so I really need you to come today and fix this. I don't want people to see the yard looking so bad, and I certainly don't want you guys coming during the party.

嗨。我是東尼・馬汀內斯。我住在亨丁頓那邊的楓樹街 124 號。你們的員工通常會在星期二來修剪我家的草坪，但是上週二卻沒有人過來…我猜是因為那天下雨。無論如何，他們終於在昨天過來修剪了，但是他們忘記修剪後院的某一區。那裡看起來真的很糟，因為下雨加上其他原因，使得那邊雜草叢生。而我們將在明天舉辦一個大型的戶外派對，所以我非常需要你們今天過來，解決這個問題。我不想讓別人看到我的庭院這麼糟糕，而我當然也不希望你們在派對進行時過來。

**

Tony Martinez ('tonɪ mɑr'tinɪz) *n.* 東尼・馬汀內斯

cut (kʌt) *v.* 修剪（花草）　　lawn (lɔn) *n.* 草坪

'cause (kɔz) *conj.* 因為（= *because* ）

backyard ('bæk,jɑrd) *n.* 後院　　***and all*** 以及其他一切；等等

have (hæv) *v.* 舉辦　　fix (fɪks) *v.* 處理；解決

certainly ('sɝtṇlɪ) *adv.* 一定　　***you guys*** 你們

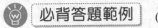 必背答題範例 (**Track 15**)

***Hello*, *Mr*. *Martinez*.**
This is Jennie at Happy Lawn Service.
I'm returning your call.

I'm very sorry that you are unhappy with the
 service you received.
I'm sure the workers did not do it on purpose.
As you said, they probably just forgot.

I understand that you need to have your lawn
 recut right away.
I'll do my best to make this happen.
Unfortunately, it is too late to send anyone today.

I suggest that we cut the lawn in the morning.
I'll send some workers to your house first thing.
They should be there by 9:00.

I will tell them what needs to be done.
The job shouldn't take long.
They'll be out of your way within half an hour.

If there is any problem tomorrow, please call me.
I'll take care of it right away.
I want to make sure you are satisfied.

中文翻譯

哈囉，馬汀內斯先生。
我是快樂草坪公司的珍妮。
我是要回覆您的電話。

對於您不滿意您所受到的服務，我很抱歉。
我相信工人們並不是故意這樣做的。
就像您所說的，他們可能只是忘記了。

我了解您需要立刻再次修剪您的草坪。
我會盡力幫您達成。
遺憾的是，現在太晚了，無法派人今天過去。

我建議我們在早上修剪草坪。
我會派工人一早就去您家裡。
他們應該在九點前就會到達。

我會告訴他們必須做什麼。
這項工作應該不會花太多時間。
他們會在半小時內離開，以免妨礙到您。

如果明天有任何問題，請打電話給我。
我會立即處理。
我希望能確保您感到滿意。

**

service〔'sɜvɪs〕*n.* 商業性服務機構；服務
return〔rɪ'tɜn〕*v.* 回覆　　unhappy〔ʌn'hæpɪ〕*adj.* 不滿意的
receive〔rɪ'siv〕*v.* 收到；受到　　***on purpose*** 故意地
recut〔rɪ'kʌt〕*v.* 再修剪　　***do one's best*** 盡力
unfortunately〔ʌn'fɔrtʃənɪtlɪ〕*adv.* 不幸地；遺憾的是
first thing 一早　　***out of one's way*** 讓開；不妨礙某人
take care of 處理　　***make sure*** 確保

Question 11 : Express an Opinion

Track 14

Directions: In this part of the test, you will give your opinion about a specific topic. Be sure to say as much as you can in the time allowed. You will have 15 seconds to prepare. Then you will have 60 seconds to speak.

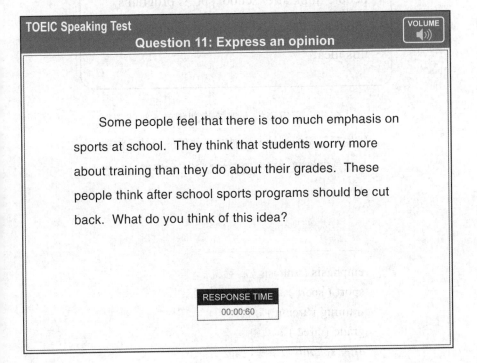

TOEIC Speaking Test

VOLUME

Question 11: Express an opinion

Some people feel that there is too much emphasis on sports at school. They think that students worry more about training than they do about their grades. These people think after school sports programs should be cut back. What do you think of this idea?

RESPONSE TIME
00:00:60

Some people feel that there is too much emphasis on sports at school. They think that students worry more about training than they do about their grades. These people think after school sports programs should be cut back. What do you think of this idea?

有些人認為學校太過於強調體育。他們認為學生關心體能訓練,勝過關心他們的成績。這些人認為課後體育活動應該被削減。你覺得這個想法如何?

** ─────────────

emphasis〔'ɛmfəsɪs〕n. 強調
sport〔sport〕n. 運動;體育活動
training〔'trenɪŋ〕n. 訓練
grade〔gred〕n. 成績
after school 放學後;課後
sports〔sports〕adj. 運動的
program〔'progræm〕n. 活動   **cut back** 削減

必背答題範例 (Track 15)

In my opinion, sports are important.

But they are not more important than education.

Students should be encouraged to keep a balance.

Practicing a sport will teach them good habits.

They can stay healthy all their lives.

They can also learn about teamwork.

After school sports are also a good way to
relieve stress.

The students can relax and make friends.

They may be able to study better afterwards.

So I don't think the sports programs should be cut.

Physical education is part of a complete education.

However, academics have to come first.

The best thing might be to require good grades.

Without good grades, the students couldn't play.

If their grades fell, they would have to stop.

This would make everybody happy.

The students would get to play sports.

And the teachers and parents would see good grades.

中文翻譯

我認爲體育是很重要的。
但是並沒有比教育重要。
應該鼓勵學生在其中取得平衡。

運動可以教導他們良好的習慣。
他們可以終其一生都保持健康。
他們也可以學到團隊合作。

課後運動也是一種減輕壓力的好方法。
學生們可以放鬆並交朋友。
之後他們唸書的效率也許會更好。

所以我認爲不應該刪減體育活動。
體育課是健全教育的一部份。
然而,學術必須擺在第一位。

最好的辦法,是要求好成績。
沒有好成績,學生就不能參加體育活動。
如果他們成績下滑,他們就必須停止。

這會讓每個人都滿意。
學生們能夠運動。
老師和家長也能看到好成績。

** ————————————————————————————

encourage〔ɪnˋkɝɪdʒ〕v. 鼓勵　　　balance〔ˋbæləns〕n. 平衡
teamwork〔ˋtimͺwɝk〕n. 團隊合作　　relieve〔rɪˋliv〕v. 減輕
stress〔strɛs〕n. 壓力 (= pressure)　　*make friends* 交朋友
afterwards〔ˋæftɚwɚdz〕adv. 之後　　*physical education* 體育課 (= PE)
complete〔kəmˋplit〕adj. 完整的　　academics〔ͺækəˋdɛmɪks〕n. 學術
come〔kʌm〕v. 位於　　*come first* 擺在第一位 (= have first priority)
play〔ple〕v. 參加體育活動　　*get to V.* 得以~

TOEIC Speaking Test ⑧

Question 1: Read a Text Aloud

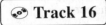 **Track 16**

Directions: In this part of the test, you will read aloud the text on the screen. You will have 45 seconds to prepare. Then you will have 45 seconds to read the text aloud.

TOEIC Speaking Test

VOLUME 🔊

Question 1: Read a text aloud

Are you about to move house? Then you have a lot to do. Let Home Movers help you. Our professional staff will pack, load and transport your belongings to your new home, all without a scratch. Home Movers is fully insured against damage and has an excellent reputation. So relax, and let us do the heavy lifting.

RESPONSE TIME
00:00:45

題目解說 (**Track 17**)

> Are you about to move house? Then you have a lot to do. Let Home Movers help you. Our professional staff will pack, load and transport your belongings to your new home, all without a scratch. Home Movers is fully insured against damage and has an excellent reputation. So relax, and let us do the heavy lifting.

你要搬家嗎？那你有很多事要做。讓搬家公司來幫你。我們的專業人員會將你的物品打包、裝載，然後運送到你的新家，完全不會有任何擦撞。搬家公司有完整的損害保險和良好的聲譽。所以放輕鬆，讓我們來做粗重的搬運工作。

** ─────────────

be about to V. 將要⋯　　***move house*** 搬家
movers﹝'muvɚz﹞*n.* 搬家公司
professional﹝prə'fɛʃənl̩﹞*adj.* 專業的
staff﹝stæf﹞*n.* 工作人員　　pack﹝pæk﹞*v.* 打包
load﹝lod﹞*v.* 裝載　　transport﹝træns'port﹞*v.* 運送
belongings﹝bə'lɔŋɪŋz﹞*n. pl.* 所有物；財產
scratch﹝skrætʃ﹞*n.* 刮痕
insured﹝ɪn'ʃʊrd﹞*adj.* 已投保的
damage﹝'dæmɪdʒ﹞*n.* 損壞
reputation﹝ˌrɛpjə'teʃən﹞*n.* 名聲
lift﹝lɪft﹞*v.* 運送；抬起；舉起

Question 2 : Read a Text Aloud

Track 16

Directions: In this part of the test, you will read aloud the text on the screen. You will have 45 seconds to prepare. Then you will have 45 seconds to read the text aloud.

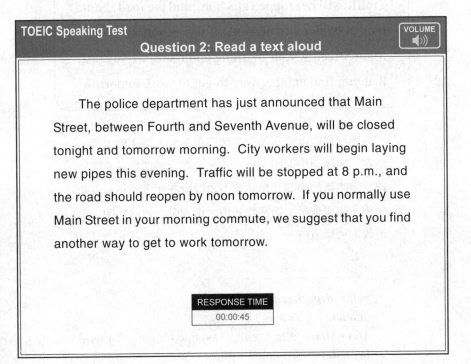

TOEIC Speaking Test

Question 2: Read a text aloud

VOLUME

The police department has just announced that Main Street, between Fourth and Seventh Avenue, will be closed tonight and tomorrow morning. City workers will begin laying new pipes this evening. Traffic will be stopped at 8 p.m., and the road should reopen by noon tomorrow. If you normally use Main Street in your morning commute, we suggest that you find another way to get to work tomorrow.

RESPONSE TIME
00:00:45

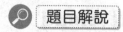

The police department has just announced that Main Street, between Fourth and Seventh Avenue, will be closed tonight and tomorrow morning. City workers will begin laying new pipes this evening. Traffic will be stopped at 8 p.m., and the road should reopen by noon tomorrow. If you normally use Main Street in your morning commute, we suggest that you find another way to get to work tomorrow.

警察局剛剛宣布，介於第四與第七大道間的大街，將在今晚和明早關閉。市府工人會在今晚開始舖設新管線。道路將於晚間八點封閉，預計會在明天中午前重新開放。如果你早上通常都利用大街通勤，建議你明天上班改走別條道路。

**

police department 警察局
announce〔ə'naʊns〕v. 宣布
Main Street 大街；主街　　avenue〔'ævə,nju〕n. 大道
lay〔le〕v. 舖　　pipe〔paɪp〕n. 管子
traffic〔'træfɪk〕n. 交通　　stop〔stɑp〕v. 使中斷
reopen〔ri'opən〕v. 重新開放
normally〔'nɔrml̩ɪ〕adv. 通常
commute〔kə'mjut〕n. 通勤　　*get to work* 去上班

Question 3 : Describe a Picture

Track 16

Directions: In this part of the test, you will describe the picture on your screen in as much detail as you can. You will have 30 seconds to prepare your response. Then you will have 45 seconds to speak about the picture.

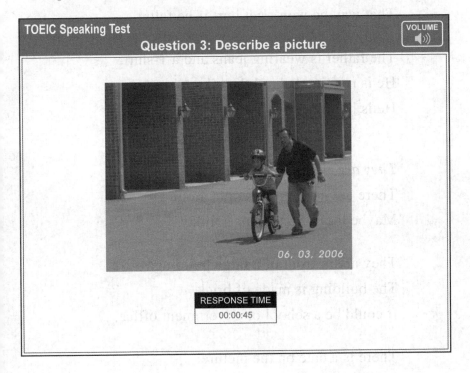

TOEIC Speaking Test

VOLUME

Question 3: Describe a picture

06, 03, 2006

RESPONSE TIME

00:00:45

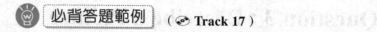

This is a picture of a father and son.
The father is teaching his son how to ride a bike.
He's pushing the bike from behind.

The boy looks about five or six years old.
He is wearing a helmet.
That way he won't get hurt if he falls.

The father is wearing jeans and a T-shirt.
He is running behind the bike.
He is holding on to the seat.

They are riding in an empty place.
There are no cars or people around.
Maybe it is a Sunday or holiday.

They are in front of a large building.
The building is made of brick.
It could be a school or government office.

There is a date on the picture.
It says June 3, 2006.
Maybe the boy's mother took the picture.

中文翻譯

這是一張父親和兒子的照片。
父親正在教兒子如何騎腳踏車。
他正從後面推腳踏車。

男孩看起來大約五、六歲。
他戴著安全帽。
這樣他跌倒時就不會受傷了。

父親穿著牛仔褲和 T 恤。
他在腳踏車後面跑。
他緊抓著座椅。

他們在一個空曠的地方騎車。
四周沒有汽車或人。
或許那天是星期天或假日。

他們在一棟大型建築物前面。
建築物是以磚塊砌成的。
它可能是學校或政府機關。

照片上有日期。
上面寫著二〇〇六年六月三日。
也許是男孩的媽媽照了這張照片。

** ────────────────────

helmet〔ˈhɛlmɪt〕*n.* 安全帽　　***that way*** 那樣
get hurt 受傷　　jeans〔dʒinz〕*n.* 牛仔褲
T-shirt〔ˈtiˌʃɜt〕*n.* T 恤　　***hold on to*** 緊抓
building〔ˈbɪldɪŋ〕*n.* 建築物
be made of 由⋯製成　　brick〔brɪk〕*n.* 磚頭
government〔ˈgʌvɚnmənt〕*n.* 政府　　say〔se〕*v.* 寫著

Questions 4-6 : Respond to Questions

> **Track 16**

Directions: In this part of the test, you will answer three questions. For each question, begin responding immediately after you hear a beep. No preparation time is provided. You will have 15 seconds to respond to Questions 4 and 5 and 30 seconds to respond to Question 6.

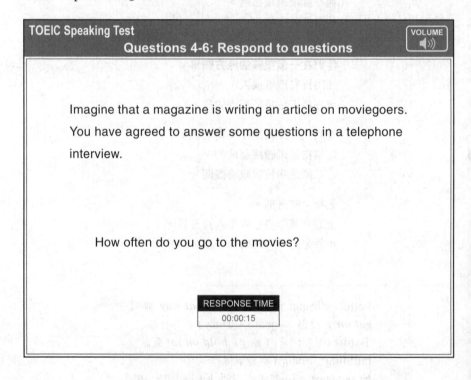

TOEIC Speaking Test	VOLUME
Questions 4-6: Respond to questions	

Imagine that a magazine is writing an article on moviegoers. You have agreed to answer some questions in a telephone interview.

How often do you go to the movies?

RESPONSE TIME
00:00:15

⇨ Question 5 is on the next page.

 **Track 16**

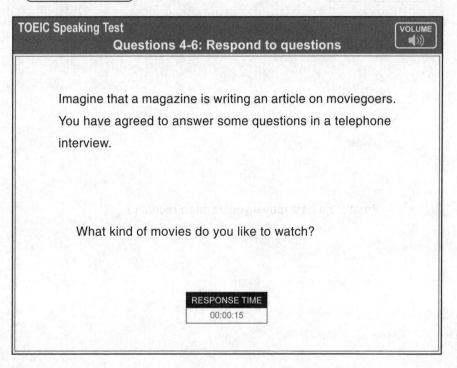

TOEIC Speaking Test
Questions 4-6: Respond to questions

VOLUME

Imagine that a magazine is writing an article on moviegoers.
You have agreed to answer some questions in a telephone
interview.

What kind of movies do you like to watch?

RESPONSE TIME
00:00:15

⇨ Question 6 is on the next page.

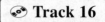

Track 16

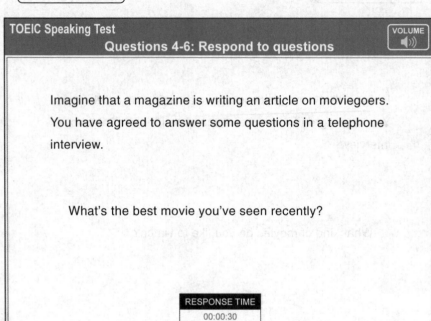

TOEIC Speaking Test
Questions 4-6: Respond to questions

VOLUME

Imagine that a magazine is writing an article on moviegoers.
You have agreed to answer some questions in a telephone
interview.

What's the best movie you've seen recently?

RESPONSE TIME
00:00:30

必背答題範例 （ Track 17 ）

Imagine that a magazine is writing an article on moviegoers. You have agreed to answer some questions in a telephone interview.

想像一下，有本雜誌正在撰寫一篇有關常看電影的人的文章。你已同意於電話訪問中回答一些問題。

Q4: How often do you go to the movies?
你多久去看一次電影？

A4: I go to the movies around once a month.
我大約一個月去看一次電影。
I go more often during holidays.
我比較常在假日時去。
There are a lot of good films out then.
那時會有許多好電影上映。

Q5: What kind of movies do you like to watch?
你喜歡看什麼樣的電影？

A5: I like many kinds of movies. 我喜歡很多種電影。
But my favorites are sci-fi and fantasy.
但是我最喜歡的是科幻和奇幻類。
I love the special effects. 我喜歡特效。

** ———————————————

moviegoer (ˈmuvɪˌgoɚ) *n.* 常看電影的人
interview (ˈɪntɚˌvju) *n.* 訪問　　around (əˈraʊnd) *adv.* 大約
film (fɪlm) *n.* 電影　　out (aʊt) *adv.* 發表；問世
favorite (ˈfevərɪt) *n.* 最喜愛的人或物
sci-fi (ˈsaɪˈfaɪ) *n.* 科幻小說 (= *science fiction*)
fantasy (ˈfæntəsɪ) *n.* 幻想
special effects （電影等的）特殊效果

Q6： What's the best movie you've seen recently?
　　 你最近看過最棒的電影是哪一部？

A6： I just saw *The 300*.
　　 It's about ancient Greece.
　　 It's about a famous battle.

　　 There is a lot of sword fighting.
　　 There are some exciting scenes.
　　 But it's very violent.

　　 Actually, the story wasn't that special.
　　 But the special effects were amazing.
　　 Almost everything was done by computer.

我剛看過三百壯士。
是關於古希臘的故事。
是關於一場有名的戰役。

有很多刀光劍影的打鬥場面。
有幾幕刺激的場景。
但是非常暴力。

事實上，故事並不特別。
但是特效非常驚人。
幾乎所有畫面都是由電腦完成的。

** ─────────────────────

recently〔ˈrisṇtlɪ〕 *adv.* 最近
ancient〔ˈenʃənt〕 *adj.* 古代的　　Greece〔gris〕 *n.* 希臘
famous〔ˈfeməs〕 *adj.* 有名的　　battle〔ˈbætḷ〕 *n.* 戰役
sword〔sord〕 *n.* 劍　　fighting〔ˈfaɪtɪŋ〕 *n.* 戰鬥
scene〔sin〕 *n.* 場景　　violent〔ˈvaɪələnt〕 *adj.* 暴力的
actually〔ˈæktʃʊəlɪ〕 *adv.* 事實上　　that〔ðæt〕 *adv.* 那麼

Questions 7-9 : Respond to Questions Using Information Provided

Track 16

TOEIC Speaking Test
Questions 7-9: Respond to questions using information provided

Directions: In this part of the test, you will answer three questions based on the information provided. You will have 30 seconds to read the information before the questions begin. For each question, begin responding immediately after you hear a beep. No additional preparation time is provided. You will have 15 seconds to respond to Questions 7 and 8 and 30 seconds to respond to Question 9.

TOEIC Speaking Test

Questions 7-9: Respond to questions using information provided

VOLUME

Easy Credit

If you have been denied a credit card, talk to us about our easy requirements.

Easy Credit cardholders must be:

> - 18 or older
> - A resident of Illinois
> - Employed full- or part-time
> - In possession of a valid driver's license

To apply: Visit our offices at 123 Main St.

Open from 8 a.m.-3 p.m., Monday-Friday

Or fill out an online application at www.easycredit.com

For more information call 1-800-329-EASY

Annual interest rate: 25%, no minimum payment required

Credit limit: $250 - $1000

題目解說

【中文翻譯】

放鬆信貸

如果你曾申請信用卡被拒，來和我們聊聊我們簡易的申請條件。

放鬆信貸的持卡人必須爲：

➤ 18 歲以上
➤ 伊利諾州居民
➤ 有全職或兼職工作
➤ 擁有有效的駕照

申請方式：請親洽我們位於大街 123 號的辦公室
營業時間爲早上八點到下午三點，週一至週五

或者到 www.easycredit.com 填寫線上申請表格

要了解更多資訊，請電 1-800-329-EASY

年利率：25%，無最低應繳金額
信用額度：250 美元 - 1000 美元

【背景敘述】

> Hello. I saw your advertisement for a credit card. I'd like to apply for it. I'd like some more information.

哈囉。我看見你們的信用卡廣告。我想要申請。我想獲得更多的資訊。

** ———————————————

easy〔'izɪ〕*adj.* 輕鬆的；容易的；不苛求的
credit〔'krɛdɪt〕*n.* 信用；貸款　***easy credit*** 放鬆信貸
deny〔dɪ'naɪ〕*v.* 拒絕給予　***credit card*** 信用卡
requirements〔rɪ'kwaɪrmənts〕*n. pl.* 必備條件；要求
cardholder〔'kard,holdə〕*n.* 持卡人
resident〔'rɛzədənt〕*n.* 居民
Illinois〔,ɪlə'nɔɪ , ,ɪlə'nɔɪz〕*n.* 伊利諾州
full-time〔'fʊl'taɪm〕*adv.* 全職地
part-time〔'part'taɪm〕*adv.* 兼職地

in possession of 擁有　　valid〔'vælɪd〕*adj.* 有效的
license〔'laɪsn̩s〕*n.* 執照　***a driver's license*** 汽車駕照
apply〔ə'plaɪ〕*v.* 申請　***fill out*** 填寫
online〔'an,laɪn〕*adj.* 線上的；網路上的
application〔,æplə'keʃən〕*n.* 申請書
annual〔'ænjʊəl〕*adj.* 一年的　　interest〔'ɪntrɪst〕*n.* 利息
interest rate 利率　　minimum〔'mɪnəməm〕*adj.* 最小的
payment〔'pemənt〕*n.* 支付金額
limit〔'lɪmɪt〕*n.* 限制；限度　***credit limit*** 信用額度
advertisement〔,ædvə'taɪzmənt〕*n.* 廣告

必背答題範例 (**Track 17**)

Q7: I'm 19, but I live with my parents. Can I still get a card?

我十九歲，但我和父母同住。我能申請信用卡嗎？

A7: Yes, you can.

You're a resident of Illinois.

But you also need to have a job.

是的，你可以。

你是伊利諾州居民。

但你還需要有一份工作。

Q8: How much can I buy with the card?

我可以用信用卡買多少錢的東西？

A8: Your credit limit will be at least $250.

It might be as high as $1000.

It depends on how much money you earn.

你的信用額度至少有二百五十美元。

最高一千美元。

視你所賺的錢而定。

** ─────────────

at least 至少　　***depend on*** 視～而定

earn〔ɝn〕*v.* 賺（錢）

Q9: Can I apply over the phone?
　　我可以用電話申請嗎？

A9: No, you can't.
　　There are two ways to apply.
　　You can do it in person or online.

　　You can come into our office.
　　We're open Monday through Friday.
　　Come between eight and three.

　　You can also apply online.
　　Just go to our website.
　　The form is easy to fill out.

　　不，你不能。
　　有兩種申請辦法。
　　你可以親自申請或線上申請。

　　你可以來我們的辦公室。
　　我們從週一營業到週五。
　　要在八點至三點之間過來。

　　你也可以線上申請。
　　只要去我們的網站。
　　表格填寫相當容易。

** ————————————————————

over the phone 用電話 (= *on the phone*)
in person 親自　　online〔'ɑn,laɪn〕*adv.* 在線上
through〔θru〕*prep.*（從…）到～為止
website〔'wɛb,saɪt〕*n.* 網站
form〔fɔrm〕*n.* 表格

Question 10 : Propose a Solution

Track 16

Directions: In this part of the test, you will be presented with a problem and asked to propose a solution. You will have 30 seconds to prepare. Then you will have 60 seconds to speak. In your response, be sure to show that you recognize the problem, and propose a way of dealing with the problem.

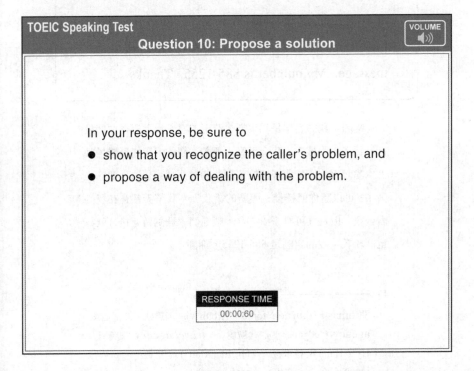

TOEIC Speaking Test
VOLUME
Question 10: Propose a solution

In your response, be sure to
- show that you recognize the caller's problem, and
- propose a way of dealing with the problem.

RESPONSE TIME
00:00:60

➡ Now listen to the voice message.

【語音留言】

> Hello. My name is Thomas Filburne. I bought
> a ticket from your travel agency last week. I'm
> flying to New York this evening. My flight leaves at
> 6 p.m., but I can't seem to find my ticket. I'm afraid
> I've lost it. Can you issue a new one for me? I'll be
> at my office all day, but I can send someone over to
> pick it up. Please call me as soon as you get this
> message. My number is 885-1255. Thanks.

　　哈囉。我的名字是湯瑪斯・菲爾伯恩。我上週在你們旅行社買了一張機票。我今天晚上要飛往紐約。我的班機是晚上六點起飛,但是我好像找不到我的機票。我恐怕是把它弄丟了。可以請你們補發一張新的給我嗎?我整天都會在我的辦公室,但是我可以派人去拿。請你們一聽到留言後,就打電話給我。我的電話是 885-1255。謝謝。

** ────────────────

Thomas Filburne ('tɑməs 'fɪlbɜn) *n.* 湯瑪斯・菲爾伯恩
agency ('edʒənsɪ) *n.* 代辦處　　*travel agency* 旅行社
fly (flaɪ) *v.* 搭飛機　　flight (flaɪt) *n.* 班機
issue ('ɪʃu) *v.* 發出　　*pick up* 拿
message ('mɛsɪdʒ) *n.* 訊息;留言

必背答題範例 (Track 17)

Hello, Mr. Filburne.
This is Donna at Fly Right Travel.
I'm returning your call.

I got your message about your ticket.
I'm working on the problem right now.
We're going to reissue the ticket today.

Luckily, we have a record of your ticket number.
The airline has agreed to cancel it.
They're going to provide a new one.

It's going to take a little time to do this.
We may not have the ticket for you in time.
I suggest you pick it up at the airport.

The airline can issue it right there.
Just go to their ticket office.
But try to get there a little early.

I don't think you'll have any trouble.
If you have any questions, give me a call.
I'll be in the office until 7:00 tonight.

中文翻譯

哈囉，菲爾伯恩先生。
我是飛睿旅行社的唐娜。
我是要回覆您的電話。

我收到了您有關機票的留言。
我現在正在處理這個問題。
我們會在今天補發機票。

幸運的是，我們有您機票號碼的記錄。
航空公司已經同意取消它。
他們會提供新號碼。

這個過程會花一點時間。
我們可能無法及時為您拿到機票。
我建議您到機場取票。

航空公司可以當場補發。
只要到他們的售票處。
但是請試著早一點到達。

我想您應該不會有任何問題。
如果您有任何疑問，請打電話給我。
我今晚會在辦公室待到七點。

**

return〔rɪˈtɜn〕v. 回覆　　　***work on*** 致力於
reissue〔riˈɪʃu〕v. 再發出　　　record〔ˈrɛkəd〕n. 記錄
airline〔ˈɛr͵laɪn〕n. 航空公司　　cancel〔ˈkænsl̩〕v. 取消
provide〔prəˈvaɪd〕v. 提供　　　***in time*** 及時
ticket office 售票處　　***give*** sb. ***a call*** 打電話給某人

Question 11 : Express an Opinion

Track 16

Directions: In this part of the test, you will give your opinion about a specific topic. Be sure to say as much as you can in the time allowed. You will have 15 seconds to prepare. Then you will have 60 seconds to speak.

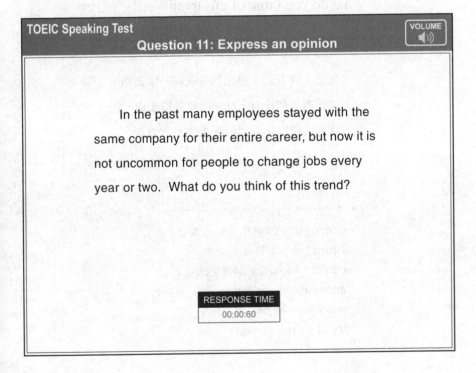

TOEIC Speaking Test
Question 11: Express an opinion

VOLUME

In the past many employees stayed with the same company for their entire career, but now it is not uncommon for people to change jobs every year or two. What do you think of this trend?

RESPONSE TIME
00:00:60

題目解說

> In the past many employees stayed
> with the same company for their entire
> career, but now it is not uncommon for
> people to change jobs every year or two.
> What do you think of this trend?

　　過去，許多員工終生都待在同一家公司，
但是現在對人們而言，每一兩年就換工作，已
經是常有的情況。你對這種趨勢有何看法？

** ────────────

employee〔͵ɛmplɔɪˈi〕*n.* 受雇者；員工
entire〔ɪnˈtaɪr〕*adj.* 全部的
career〔kəˈrɪr〕*n.* 職業生涯
uncommon〔ʌnˈkɑmən〕*adj.* 罕見的
every year or two 每一兩年
trend〔trɛnd〕*n.* 趨勢

I think this trend is a good thing for many people.
It forces them to keep their skills sharp.
They have to stay competitive.

You can also learn a lot by working in different
  places.
You meet new colleagues.
You hear new ideas.

Companies also have to compete for the best
  employees.
They have to offer good compensation.
They have to challenge people and promote them.

Of course, there is also a downside.
There is less security when people move around
  a lot.
This is true for both the workers and the companies.

Employees can't build up good relationships.
They have to spend a lot of their time adapting.
And they're always looking for the next job.

Companies have a high staff turnover.
This can be bad for business.
They constantly have to train new people.

中文翻譯

我想這個趨勢對很多人來說是好事。
它促使人們維持精湛的技能。
他們必須保持競爭力。

在不同的地方工作,也可以學到很多。
可以認識新同事。
可以聽到新的想法。

公司也必須爭取最棒的員工。
它們必須提供優渥的薪水。
它們必須考驗員工的能力,並讓他們升遷。

當然,這也是有缺點。
當人們經常更換工作時,會比較沒有安全感。
這對員工和公司來說,都是如此。

員工們無法建立良好的關係。
他們必須花很多時間適應。
而且他們永遠都在尋找下一份工作。

公司的員工流動率會很高。
這對企業來說並不是好事。
他們必須不斷訓練新人。

** ———————————————————

sharp〔ʃɑrp〕*adj.* 敏銳的;厲害的
competitive〔kəm'pɛtətɪv〕*adj.* 有競爭力的
compensation〔ˌkɑmpən'seʃən〕*n.* 薪水
challenge〔'tʃælɪndʒ〕*v.* 考驗(…的能力)
promote〔prə'mot〕*v.* 使升遷   downside〔'daʊn'saɪd〕*n.* 缺點
security〔sɪ'kjʊrətɪ〕*n.* 安全感   *move around* 經常更換工作
build up 建立   adapt〔ə'dæpt〕*v.* 適應
staff〔stæf〕*n.* 工作人員   turnover〔'tɜn,ovə〕*n.* 人事變動率

「TOEIC 口說測驗」該怎麼教？

1. 在「TOEIC 口說測驗」中的第一題和第二題，是 Read a text aloud（朗讀一段文章），text 一般當「原文」解，在這裡作 a passage（一段文章）解。

首先老師要了解停頓的原則：

(1) 依照標點符號而停頓

標點符號如句點（Full Stop）、逗點（Comma）、問號（Interrogation Mark）、感嘆號（Exclamation Mark）、半支點（Semicolon）、長劃（Dash）等，通常都自然成為意群（Thought Group）區分的界限。以下用斜線 / 表示停頓。

> a beautiful, / young girl
> Elizabeth, / come this way.
> Yes, / I'll.
> No, / it won't do.
> All right, / I'll go with you.
> There was nothing for it / but to go back as I had come— /
> on foot.（— 為長劃）
> Generally speaking, / they are good students.
> "We will send somebody." "Who? / When? / Where to?"
> There! / There! / Don't cry.
> You are, / to speak the truth, / afraid of the enemy.

※ 注意下列例外：

(A) 省略號不停頓

P.O.O.（= post-office order）　　Dr. Brown

(B) 表示單位的標點不停頓

$2.20（二元二角）　　8:10 A.M.（上午八點十分）

⒞ 代名詞和同位語之間的逗點不停頓

We, Chinese people, / are peace-loving people.

⒟ 簡短回答有 **sir** 時，不停頓

Yes, sir.　　　　Here, sir.　　　　No, sir.

⒠ 感嘆詞和稱呼主格可不停頓

Oh, Mother, / what shall I do?

⑵ 名詞以及在它前面的修飾語構成一單位

the teacher　　　a dog　　　　an American

two books　　　my new knife　　an intimate friend

beautiful house　　black paper　　the damaged car

⑶ 介詞片語在句中構成一單位

They lived / in a beautiful house / near a wood.

First of all, / plant needs water / for its growth.

⑷ 疑問詞 + 不定詞；**how** + 形容詞、副詞或現在分詞構成一單位

how to swim　　　how beautiful　　how pleasing

⑸ 動詞片語構成一單位

will come　　could go　　are eating　　must have done

⑹ 代名詞和動詞（片語）構成一單位

I went.　　　　　Do you see?　　　He can write.

She weeps.　　　They are coming.　　We should eat / to live.

⑺ （代名詞）動詞與補語構成一單位

I am familiar / with this story.

He is a man / who loves the truth.

⑻ 名詞子句構成一單位

That he loved her / was certain.

It was certain / that he loved her.

I think it certain / that he will succeed.

⑼ 引句獨立構成一單位

John asked, / "What time shall I come?"

"Dinner will be served at seven," / replied Mary.

⑽ 連接詞和它後面接的詞語構成一單位

Sam enjoys tennis, / golf, / and baseball.

You can go to Hualien by bus, / or by boat, / or by airplane.

He gave me money / as well as advice.

Edison is an inventor / whose fame is worldwide.

I will come / when I am at leisure.

She wept aloud / as soon as she heard the news.

　　老師在教 Question 1 和 Question 2　Read a text aloud 的時候，可以先停下來，給學生 45 秒鐘的時間，自己小聲唸一唸，用鉛筆劃線。

　　老師教的時候，一面唸，一面翻成中文，到停頓的時候，叫同學劃斜線。例如：

Did you know / that riding a bicycle / for as little as
/ half an hour a day / —around five miles— / can cut your
risk / of developing heart disease / in half? / Not only that, /
but cycling / is a lot less expensive / than driving your car, /
not to mention / pollution-free. / So / why not ride / to work
today? / You can do something good / for your heart, / your
pocketbook / and the environment / all at the same time.

Did you know 先說「你知道嗎」，然後說「劃斜線」，對於學生困惑的地方，你要強調，像 Did you know that riding a bicycle... 學生不知道要唸 Did you know 或 Did you know that 後要停頓，此時你就要說明，連接詞和它後面的詞語構成一單位，所以停頓應該停在 know 的後面。可以寫在黑板上：

Did you know / that riding a bicycle...
連接詞和它後面的詞語構成一個單位

再說：that riding a bicycle...miles can, riding a bicycle...miles 是動名詞片語當主詞，由於主詞很長，要停頓，即使是介詞片語，很長也要停頓。最好是一面上課、一面說，帶著同學一面唸。同學如果不唸，可重複叫他們再唸。如：for as little as 可重複兩遍以上，**一定要訓練學生，養成上課時跟你唸的習慣**。

2. 「TOEIC 口說測驗」中 Question 3 的「描述圖片」（Describe a picture）該怎麼教呢？

┌─「描述圖片」的公式：─────────────
│ ① 說出這是什麼地方　　④ 說出次要人物他們在做什麼
│ ② 說出主要人物　　　　⑤ 如果有標語，可利用標語造句
│ ③ 說出他在做什麼　　　⑥ 說出自己的感覺
└──────────────────────────

例如：

首先說出這是什麼地方。告訴同學，下面這三句話像是一個公式，看到什麼圖片，都可用它來造句。

> ***This is*** an airport.（這是機場。）【用 This is 造句】
> ***It's a picture of*** a terminal.（這是航空站的照片。）
> 【用 It's a picture of 來造句】
> ***It looks like*** a large one.（看起來是座很大的航空站。）
> 【用 It looks like 來造句，並說出自己的感覺】

由於要講 45 秒，至少必須講 18 句，以三句為一組。

> ***It's*** a long narrow hall.（這是條長而狹窄的走廊。）
> 【用 It's 來造句，描述地點】
> ***It's*** brightly lit.（光線很充足。）【用 It's 來造句，描述燈光】
> ***It looks*** very clearn.（看起來非常乾淨。）【用 It looks 說出自己的感覺】

裡面有難的單字，必須寫在黑板上，像 terminal〔ˈtɜmənl〕 *n.* 航空站，lit 是 light 的過去分詞，都要清楚地寫在黑板上。

地點描述完後，換描述人物。描述人物時，要先描述主要人物，說明他們正在做什麼，也可以說出自己的感覺，推測他們接下來會做的事。行有餘力的話，再描述其他次要人物。

> ***There are*** many people.（有很多人。）
> 【用 There are 來造句，說出圖片中的人物】
> Some are on a moving walkway.（有些在電動走道上。）
> 【說明他們在哪裡】
> They're headed to their gates.（他們正前往他們的登機門。）
> 【說出他們在做什麼】

若圖片中有標誌，就可以利用標誌來造句。可以將標誌中的重點字應用到句子裡，例如此題中的 gate（登機門）和 hotel（旅館）。如果標誌中有看不懂的字，就不要用，但是老師上課時，還是必須將這些生字告訴學生。

There are many signs. (有很多標誌。)

【用 There are 來造句，指出圖片中有標誌】

They direct people to the gates. (它們引導人們前往登機門。)

They show the way to the hotel. (它們指出前往旅館的方向。)

【用 They 來造句，說明標誌的用途】

考試時要仔細觀察圖片，找出值得描述的次要景物。當主要地點和人物都描述完後，就可以派上用場。

There are some shops, too. (還有一些商店。)

【用 There are 來造句，說出圖片裡的次要景物】

They sell magazines and snacks. (它們販賣雜誌和點心。)

They're convenient for travelers. (它們對旅客來說很方便。)

【用 They 來造句，描述次要景物】

如果最後還有多餘的時間，可以說說自己對照片中人、事、物的感覺。

No one appears to be in a hurry. (沒有人顯得匆忙。)

【說出自己的感覺】

They have plenty of time to spare. (他們有很多多餘的時間。)

They're relaxed and happy. (他們輕鬆而愉快。)

講解完答題技巧後，一定要帶著同學全部再多唸幾遍。多益口說的考題總共有十一題，愈到後面，挑戰性愈高。老師可以將第 3 題當作暖身，**讓同學習慣三句一組、九句一段的回答方式**，以後回答第 4 到第 11 題時，就容易了。

3. 「TOEIC 口說測驗」中，Questions 4-6「回答問題」(Respond to questions) 會怎麼考？

　　Questions 4-6「回答問題」(Respond to questions) 是一個題組。電腦會設定一個與日常生活有關的情境，然後請考生依據這個情境，以自身的經驗，回答三個問題。

例如：

Imagine that a radio station is doing some research on its listeners.
You have agreed to answer some questions in a telephone interview.
（想像一下，有家廣播電台正在對聽眾進行調查。你已同意於電話訪問
中回答一些問題。）

Q4: When are you most likely to listen to the radio?
　　（你最有可能在何時聽廣播？）

Q5: Have you ever called in to a live radio program?
　　（你是否曾打電話到現場直播的廣播節目？）

Q6: Would you rather listen to an all-music station or one that features
　　a lot of conversation?
　　（你喜歡收聽只播音樂的電台，還是以講話為主的電台？）

在教授答題技巧前，老師務必提醒學生兩件事：
① 這個題組的每個問題，在考生回答之前，都沒有提供準備時間。
② 每題的回答時間不相同：第 4 及第 5 題為 15 秒，第 6 題 30 秒。

4. 那麼該怎麼教 Questions 4-6「回答問題」（Respond to questions）？

　　　Questions 4-6 的得分要訣，就是採用「**開門見山法**」來回答。一開
始就要回答到重點，然後再把握多餘時間，多加敘述補充。

　　　第 4 及第 5 題為相同題型，故我們僅以第 4 題的答題典範為例。由於
這兩題的答題時間短，所以最好在第一句，就直接了當地回答問題，然後
再用兩句話來做補充：

　　　　I usually listen when I'm in the car.
　　　　（我通常在車子裡聽廣播。）【直接回答問題】
　　　　It makes traffic jams more fun.
　　　　（這讓塞車時多了一點樂趣。）【補充說明 1】
　　　　The DJs can also make me laugh.
　　　　（DJ 也會令我發笑。）【補充說明 2】

回答第 6 題的原則，與前兩題相同。不同的是，4、5 題答題時間短，回答時以句子為單位：即第一句回答問題，第二、三句補充說明。第 6 題答題時間長，以三句一組為單位：**第一組回答問題，第二、三組分別說明兩個原因**，例如：

I turn on the radio mostly for the music.

（我打開收音機多半是為了聽音樂。）【直接回答問題】

I like pop and hip-hop the best.

（我最喜歡流行音樂及嘻哈音樂。）

I want to hear the latest tunes.（我想要聽最新的歌曲。）

以第一組直接回答問題。第一句就要回答到重點，接下來再用兩句話多加說明。

提出第一個原因：

But I also like the DJs.

（但我也喜歡那些 DJ。）【補充說明 1】

I like to hear their opinions.（我喜歡聽他們的見解。）

I also like their funny jokes.（我也喜歡他們有趣的笑話。）

提出第二個原因：

But I rarely listen to talk radio.

（不過我很少聽談話性節目。）【補充說明 2】

I just want to relax.（我只想要放鬆。）

I don't want to listen to the news.（我不想聽新聞。）

如果題目是叫考生在兩者中擇其一，就能在這段說出為何不選另外那個的理由。

老師可以告訴同學，雖然這個題組在答題前沒有準備時間，但事實上，同學平常就可以準備了！這個題組都是針對生活中的事物來發問，同學平常就要多涉獵與日常生活相關的英文會話，考試時，就能在短時間內反應，盡情發表意見。

5. 「TOEIC 口說測驗」中，Questions 7-9「依據題目資料應答」（Respond to questions using information provided）會怎麼考？

　　Questions 7-9「依據題目資料應答」是一個題組。考生必須依照電腦給的資料，回答三個問題。這則資料可能是傳單、公告、課表等等，如下圖：

Oak Park Community Board Meeting

When: 7 p.m., Wednesday, April 12
Where: Oak Park Community Center
Topic: Widening Oak Park Road

There are strong feelings both for and against the plan. Representatives of both sides will present their views. The discussion will be followed by a vote on whether or not the community should approve the plan.

➤ **County Commissioner Leslie Brown** is for the plan. She will speak about the number of new residents in the area and the increased traffic.

➤ **Bill Riley** is against the plan. He will present the concerns that residents have about the disruption to daily life and the impact on the environment.

➤ **David Park**, an engineer from the construction company, will give us information on how long the project will take to complete.

　　考生有三十秒的時間閱讀。三十秒後，電腦會播放一段敘述，內容是某個人打電話給你，請教你這則資料的相關問題。在回答這三題之前，都沒有準備時間，但是螢幕上會持續顯示這個資料。考生有 15 秒的時間，回答第 7 及第 8 題；30 秒的時間，回答第 9 題。

6. 那麼該怎麼教 Questions 7-9「依據題目資料應答」（Respond to questions using information provided）？

⑴ 教授閱讀資料的技巧

想在這個題組拿高分，同學不只要會說，還要會抓資料裡的重點。Questions 7-9 會考的不外是：① **何時**（when）、② **何地**（where）、③ **和什麼人有關**（who）以及④ **什麼事情**（what）。介紹完這四個出題重點後，老師可以仿照考試方式，給同學 30 秒的時間閱讀，訓練同學抓重點的能力。

⑵ 講解題目資料

同學看完後，老師要從頭開始，仔細講解這篇資料。Questions 7-9 的資料，通常是公告、傳單、時間表等，非常生活化的東西。裡面的某些情境或用語，對台灣學生來說，並不是那麼地熟悉。老師必須確實了解每個字的意思，才能告訴學生。有任何不確定的地方，都要問過外國人才可以。

⑶ 播放試題

應試時，第 7 到第 9 題的問題，都是在耳機中播放，不會顯示在螢幕上。所以老師講解完資料後，要叫同學不要翻到下一頁，專心聽你接下來要播放的內容，並且要提醒學生，注意聽題目中的疑問詞（when、where、who、what）。

⑷ 講解答題技巧

第 7 及第 8 題的回答時間只有 15 秒，只要按照螢幕上的資訊，用**簡單的直述句**回答，就可以拿到不錯的分數。例如：

Q7: When is the meeting going to be held and what time will it start?（請問會議將於何時舉行，幾點開始？）

A7: It's on April twelfth.（在四月十二日。）

That's next Wednesday.（那是下個禮拜三。）

It'll start at seven.（將會在七點開始。）

第 9 題的考試題型有三種：

① 問人物、時間、地點：這樣的題型，通常會出現在第 7 與第 8 題。如果出現在第 9 題，考生就必須多補充相關的細節。

② 要求考生敘述一部份的資訊：例如給考生某個活動的行程表，要求考生敘述整個早上、或整個下午包含哪些行程。

③ 應用題：例如給考生一張職能進修的課程表，然後問考生，如果想學習電腦技能，可以上哪些課。

不管是哪一種題型，第 9 題都可以用這樣的方法來解題：

① **列出問題的答案**
② **每個答案多用兩句補充說明**

以剛才的會議公告為例，題目問你：Who is going to speak at the meeting?（誰會在會議中發言呢？）首先列出問題的答案，發言的有：Leslie Brown、Bill Riley 和 David Park。接著每個答案多用兩句補充說明，於是我們的第一段就是：

　　Leslie Brown will speak.（雷絲麗・布朗會發言。）
　　【以簡單的直述句回答】
　　She is a county commissioner.（她是郡政委員。）
　　She is for the plan.（她支持這項計畫。）
　　【用 She is 來造句，補充說明】

然後再以同樣的方式，說出另外兩位發言人。

第 9 題的回答時間有 30 秒，考生最少要說九句。告訴學生，平常就可以多練習用三句話來說明一個主題。看到什麼東西、事物，就試著用三句話來描述。習慣了之後，對學生考試很有幫助。一來可以讓學生在考試時，言之有物，又能幫助學生，在時間壓力及緊張的情緒下，有系統、有條理地回答問題。

7. 多益口說測驗的 Question 10「提出解決方案」(Propose a solution)，
要求考生針對一段語音留言，提出解決辦法。告訴學生，聽取留言時，
要記下**留言者的姓名或稱呼方式**，以及**留言者所提出的問題**。

> 「提出解決方案」的公式：
>
> ① 開場問候　　　　　　　④ 提出解決方案
> ② 重述留言者的問題　　　⑤ 結尾
> ③ 安撫留言者，或解釋造成的原因

我們舉一個例子，來說明這個公式。馬汀內斯先生打來向除草公司抱
怨，除草工人沒有將他家的草坪除乾淨。考生可以這麼回答：

Hello, Mr. Martinez. (哈囉，馬汀內斯先生。)
【以 Hello, (某先生 / 女士) 開場】
This is Jennie at Happy Lawn Service.
(我是快樂草坪公司的珍妮。) 【用 This is 造句，自我介紹】
I'm returning your call. (我是要回覆您的電話。)
【整句背下來，不需更改】

告訴同學，這三句開場問候，是萬用公式，不管什麼問題，都可以
這樣開場。

接著整理出留言者的問題，重述重點，讓評分老師知道，你聽懂留
言了。

I'm very sorry that you are unhappy with the service
you received. (對於您不滿意您所受到的服務，我很抱歉。)
【用 I'm very sorry 造句，說出留言者的問題】
I'm sure the workers did not do it on purpose.
(我相信工人們並不是故意這樣做的。)
As you said, they probably just forgot.
(就像您所說的，他們可能只是忘記了。)
【用 As you said, 造句，重述留言者的話】

說完留言者的問題，還沒說解決辦法前，可以加入一些安撫的話來做轉折，像是：Don't worry.（不用擔心。）、I'm sure we can work something out.（我確信我們可以想出解決辦法。）；或者是為公司做保證，例如：This is very unusual.（這是非常少見的。）、We rarely get complaints.（我們很少接到抱怨。）；也可以解釋問題發生的原因，比如說：The mistake is due to~.（這個錯誤是因為～。）老師可以整理一些這方面的萬用句子，三句一組讓學生背。

> *I understand* that you need to have your lawn recut right away.
>
> （我了解您需要立刻再次修剪您的草坪。）
>
> 【用 I understand 造句，說出留言者的要求】
>
> I'll do my best to make this happen.（我會盡力幫您達成。）
>
> 【整句背下來，安撫留言者】
>
> Unfortunately, it is too late to send anyone today.
>
> （遺憾的是，現在太晚了，無法派人今天過去。）
>
> 【提出可能的解決辦法】

接著提出解決方案。第 10 題在答題之前，有 30 秒的準備時間。準備時，考生就要先想好解決方案。考生可以發揮想像力，假裝自己真的是一家公司的客服人員，然後編造 1～3 個解決辦法，接著再想每個辦法的實施細節。

> *I suggest* that we cut the lawn in the morning.
>
> （我建議我們在早上修剪草坪。）
>
> 【用 I suggest 造句，說出解決方案】
>
> *I'll* send some workers to your house first thing.
>
> （我會派工人一早就去您家裡。）【用 I'll 造句，說明細節】
>
> They should be there by 9:00.
>
> （他們應該在九點前就會到達。）

I will tell them what needs to be done.
（我會告訴他們必須做什麼。）

The job shouldn't take long.（這項工作應該不會花太多時間。）

They'll be out of your way within half an hour.
（他們會在半小時內離開，以免妨礙到您。）

考試時，電腦螢幕上會有倒數時間。倒數 10 秒時，還沒講完解決方案的，要趕快收尾。講完的，就可以用下面這三句萬用結尾，來做一個完美的結束。

If there is any problem tomorrow, please call me.
（如果明天有任何問題，請打電話給我。）【結尾】

I'll take care of it right away.（我會立即處理。）

I want to make sure you are satisfied.
（我希望能確保您感到滿意。）

8. Question 11「陳述意見」（Express an opinion）要考生針對指定的議題，陳述意見並提出理由。

　　第 11 題的題型，是典型的二分法的問題。題目會要求考生二擇一，或者針對一個情形，表達贊成或反對的意見。

　　這種題型就是英文作文常出現的題型，只是這裡是要考生用講的。所以我們作答的架構，也該採用寫英文作文時的鋪陳方式，外國人才會覺得你有條理，也才能拿高分。

┌─── 「陳述意見」的架構： ──────────────┐
│ ① 表明立場　　② 說明原因　　③ 結論 │
└──────────────────────────────┘

　　我們舉個例子來說明。題目是，現在有愈來愈多的年輕人，在唸完高中後，休息一年，去旅遊或探索其他讓他們感興趣的事，之後再繼續讀大學。你認為這些年輕人的想法怎麼樣？

外國人在論述時，一開始就會把重點點出來，不像中國人，還有冒題法、破題法之類的。所以第一句就要把你的立場明明白白說清楚。

I think it's good for some people.

（我認為對某些人來說這是好的。）【用 I think 造句，直接表明立場】

They don't know what they want to do.

（他們不知道他們想要做什麼。）

They need to experience life. （他們需要去體驗人生。）

接著要說明原因和理由，來支持你的論點。

A gap year gives them time to think.

（一年的空檔給了他們時間去思考。）【原因 1】

They can explore different careers. （他們可以探索不同的職業。）

They can find out what they're good at.

（他們可以了解他們擅長的是什麼。）

They can also use the time to travel.

（他們也可以用這段時間去旅行。）【原因 2】

They can discover other cultures. （他們可以發現其他的文化。）

They can broaden their horizons. （他們可以拓展自己的眼界。）

如果學生想到的理由不多，建議學生說完理由後，也可以從反面來說說另一個選擇的缺點，或是不選它的理由，或者，也可以舉一些例子，具體說明你的論點。

Some folks think it's a waste of time.

（有些人認為這是浪費時間。）【反面論點】

These kids are just playing around. （這些孩子只是在四處遊蕩。）

Maybe they will never go back to school.

（也許他們永遠不會回到學校。）

I don't agree with that.（我不同意那種看法。）【推翻反面論點】
I think they'll come back.（我認為他們會回去。）
And they'll be more mature.（而且他們會變得更成熟。）

最後做結論。不論是英文作文，或者是用說的陳述意見，最後的結論都必須與第一段相互呼應。

They'll appreciate college more.（他們會更珍惜大學生活。）【結論】
They will be more committed to it.（他們會更用心。）
They will be better for the experience.
（他們會因為這樣的經驗而變得更好。）

9. 還有哪些注意事項要告訴學生的呢？

⑴ 多聽英文、多唸報章雜誌

多益口說測驗的評分重點之一，是發音和語調。平時有空，就要多聽多唸，常常練習說，發音和語調才會自然。此外，碰到不會唸的字，不必緊張，就用猜測的唸法，因為就算是道地的美國人，也不是每個字都會唸。

⑵ 回答要平穩流暢

另一個評分重點，是語句的輕重緩急以及流暢度。告訴學生，不必要求自己要說得一口非常快的英文。英文說得快，不等於說得好。只要按照自己習慣的速度，平穩地回答問題，不要支支吾吾、停頓太久，就能在這一項，拿到不錯的分數。

⑶ 不要太緊張、集中精神

考口說時，盡量放鬆心情，不要太緊張。輕度的緊張有助於考試，但過度緊張除了會影響表現以外，也會使考生的喉嚨緊縮，影響口說作答。除此之外，考試時不要回想前幾題答得好不好，最重要的是好好回答正在進行的題目。尤其是第7到第9題，題目必須用聽的，還有其他沒有準備時間的問題，更是需要同學集中精神，認真作答。

劉毅 TOEIC 700 分保證班

> ✓ 一次繳費，終生上課
> ✓ 學費全國最低
> ✓ 獨家研發教材（非賣品）
> ✓ 一次繳費，所有多益班皆可上課

1. 問：什麼是「TOEIC 700 分保證」？

   答：凡是報名保證班的同學，我們保證你考取 700 分。如果未達到 700 分，就可以免費一直上課，考上 700 分為止，不再另外收費，但是你必須每年至少考一次 TOEIC 測驗，考不到 700 分，可憑成績單，繼續上課，考上 700 分為止。

2. 問：你們用什麼教材？

   答：我們請資深美籍老師，根據 TOEIC 最新出題來源改編，全新試題，市面上沒有，但是考試必有雷同出現。

3. 問：「TOEIC 700 分保證班」如何收費？

   答：「TOEIC 700 分保證班」終生無限上課，僅收 19,800 元。一次繳費，所有多益班皆可上課。

4. 問：你們有什麼贈書？

   答：報名後贈送「TOEIC MODEL TEST ①～④」及聽力原文、「TOEIC 聽力測驗講義」、「TOEIC 口說測驗講義」、「TOEIC 必考字彙」、「TOEIC 文法 700 題」、「TOEIC 字彙 500 題」、「TOEIC 聽力測驗」。我們全力協助同學應試，只要有關「多益」的書籍，通通贈送給你。

5. 上課時間：

	班　　級	上　課　時　間
台北	正規班 A 班	每週一晚上 6:30～9:30
	快進度 B 班	每週日晚上 6:30～9:30
	TOEIC 寫作班	外師免費不限次數批改
	TOEIC 口說班	不限次數約定小班上課
台中	正　規　班	每週六下午 2:00～5:00

6. 問：在哪裡報名上課？

   答：台北市許昌街 17 號 6F（壽德大樓）（劉毅英文家教班高中部）☎ (02) 2389-5212
   台中市三民路三段 125 號 7 F（太平路口，加州健身中心樓上）☎ (04) 2221-8861

劉毅英文教育機構
Liu Yi English School

【企業簡介】

「劉毅英文教育機構」創立於 1971 年，包含「劉毅英文家教班」、「學習出版有限公司」，及「財團法人台北市一口氣英語教育基金會」。

「劉毅英文」是台灣最大的英文培訓機構，數十年來，每年學生人數增加，現在僅台北市一個地區，學生人數已達一萬兩千多人。劉毅老師最初以嚴格模考而著名，學生人數不斷增加，主要原因是因為每年不斷地創新、發明。

1. 1971 年，發明「高二、高三模考制度」，考完試立刻講解，下課前發還試卷。在台南一中對面，天主教堂上課，最初由劉老師的弟弟劉曉峻醫師帶 8 位台南一中高二同學來上課。

2. 1972 年，同學增加到 50 幾人，其中王主科同學考上台大醫科，他現在是台大醫院的副院長。

3. 1973 年，學生人數增加到 120 人，有 4 位同學考上台大醫科，其中台南一中的陳耀楨同學，為當年丙組榜首。

4. 1974 年，搬到台北市北門口，第一天上課，只有一位同學，他看到劉老師，嚇得要離開。劉毅老師請他坐下來，只有一個學生也拼命上課；第二週，同學增加為 3 人。

5. 1976 年，遷至「台北市信義路三段 19 號 3F」（「國際學舍」對面，現在是「大安公園」），學生增加到 400 人。

6. 1988 年，發明「一天背好 1000 個英文單字」，學生從 1200 人，增加到 1900 人。

7. 1990 年，被人騙至台北火車站前，加入「龍門補習班」，投資一千萬元，一個禮拜後，負責人說錢用完了，劉毅老師被迫主持高三重考生班務。

8. 1995 年，為重考生發明「考前魔鬼營」，讓同學一天在魔鬼營讀 15 個小時，勝過在家讀五天，全國爭相模仿。

9. 1999 年，由於「魔鬼營」被別人先註冊，不得不改名為「戰鬥營」。

10. 2000 年，發明「超級戰鬥營」，改為供應五星級飯店便當，及寬敞的座位。

11. 2003 年，發明「一口氣英語」，一舉解決學英語的困難，學生人數增加至 6000 多人。

12. 2004 年，劉毅英文高中部遷至「台北市許昌街 17 號 6F」（壽德大樓），五星級設備，學生人數增加至 8000 多人。

13. 2007 年，「兒童美語班」、「成人英語班」、「多益班」相繼成立，包含國中部，學生人數已經達一萬兩千人。

14. 2008 年 3 月 7 日，「VIP 成人英語話劇班」在「國軍藝文中心」公演成功。

15. 2008 年 5 月，台中總部正式成立。五星級設備、六星級教學，現代 E 化的教育機構。

TOEIC 口說測驗

主　　　編 / 劉　毅

發　行　所 / 學習出版有限公司　　☎ (02) 2704-5525

郵 撥 帳 號 / 0512727-2 學習出版社帳戶

登　記　證 / 局版台業 2179 號

印　刷　所 / 裕強彩色印刷有限公司

台 北 門 市 / 台北市許昌街 10 號 2 F　☎ (02) 2331-4060・2331-9209

台灣總經銷 / 紅螞蟻圖書有限公司　　☎ (02) 2795-3656

美國總經銷 / Evergreen Book Store　☎ (818) 2813622

本公司網址　www.learnbook.com.tw

電 子 郵 件　learnbook@learnbook.com.tw

書＋MP3 一片售價：新台幣三百八十元正

2008 年 8 月 1 日初版

ISBN 978-957-519-983-8